Codename: Starman

Book 2

The Sea of Moons

Books by Mack Maloney

Mack Maloney's Haunted Universe
Iron Star
Thunder Alley

Wingman *series*
The Odessa Raid

Codename: Starman *series*
The Kalashnikov Kiss

Starhawk *series*
Starhawk
Planet America
The Fourth Empire
Battle at Zero Point
Storm Over Saturn

Chopper Ops *series*
Chopper Ops
Zero Red
Shuttle Down

Strikemasters *series*
Strikemasters
Rogue War
Fulcrum

Storm Birds *series*
Desert Lightning
Thunder from Heaven
The Gathering Storm

Codename: Starman

Book 2

The Sea of Moons

Mack Maloney

SPEAKING VOLUMES, LLC
NAPLES, FLORIDA
2020

The Sea of Moons

ISBN 978-1-64540-168-1

For my fellow Dot Rat,
Bob Messia—thanks for the music

Book One

<u>Angels Aren't Cheap</u>

Chapter One

Boston

11 p.m.

Fred Friendly had just hit it big.

Early fifties, good shape, Irish pug face, but still handsome, he'd walked into Boston's Encore casino not an hour before and bought $20,000 in chips, paying with five-and ten-dollar bills.

A few spins of the roulette wheel later and he was holding close to $800,000, so much that a casino security man escorted him to the cash-out window, gave him a complimentary briefcase and offered to walk him to his car.

But Friendly declined.

Instead he stood next to the six-foot tall jewel-encrusted sculpture of Popeye in the front lobby of the casino and waited. At last, a man dressed in maroon leisurewear stepped out of the elevator, approached and gave Friendly a black business card. Written on it in red script was the name: Viktor Robotov III.

The man said in a mild Russian accent: "My employer would like you to join him in a private game."

"I'd be glad to," Friendly replied.

Five minutes later, Friendly was led into the penthouse suite atop the Encore.

It was a collection of four massive rooms, all windows and chandeliers, with an impressive view of Boston's nighttime skyline.

One room doubled as a private pub, complete with a horseshoe bar. A card table was set up nearby. Five men sat around it; several million dollars stacked on top.

Each of the five players looked like a crime boss, sharply dressed and intimidating. Their bodyguards, strategically located nearby, appeared even more frightening. But scariest of all was the thin, devilish-looking man wearing a white suit, sitting with his back to the window, the skyline beyond giving him an odd red glow. He was of indeterminate age, his face was heavily scarred. He was sweating profusely despite the room's AC blowing full blast. This was Viktor Robotov III of Moscow's Robotov crime family in Boston on business.

This would have been a daunting situation for most people, but Friendly took it in stride.

He introduced himself to each player, surprising them with an offer to shake hands. He declined a drink, cashed in his $800,000 for chips and took the seat next to Robotov.

A dealer was running the game. He explained in thick Russian that they were playing poker, five-card draw, and none of that "pussy Texas Hold'em stuff."

The first hand was dealt, Friendly got a three, a four—and three fives.

He asked for two cards, but bucking monumental odds, dropped two of the fives.

Once everyone had been dealt, the betting started in earnest. Within a minute, two million dollars' worth of chips was on the table.

The players laid down their cards. By the time it got to Robotov, two pair—jacks and queens—was the best hand. The Russian super-gangster let out a great "Ha!" and laid down, interestingly enough, three sixes.

He started to gather in the winnings, when Friendly gently interrupted him. In return for dropping the pair of fives, Friendly had picked up a two and the last six, giving him a straight, which beat three of kind. He raked in the two million in chips.

Robotov's bodyguards started to stir; he settled them down with a flick of his hand.

"You are quite lucky, my friend," he said to Friendly instead, in near-perfect English. "Do you have a secret?"

Friendly smiled. "Would you believe 'clean living?'"

Robotov did not smile back. "No, I do not," he said.

"You got a guardian angel or something?" one of the other players growled.

"Or something," Robotov said, under his breath.

Friendly won the next five hands, twice by drawing similarly unlikely inside straights, twice by drawing three like-suit cards and turning them into flushes and one by being dealt a royal straight flush in diamonds.

None of the other players were happy at this point; the bodyguards were closing in as Friendly gleefully counted his chips. Ten million dollars and change.

Two things happened next. Room service showed up with a half dozen trays bearing late night food for the players and one of the other players took a phone call. Friendly used the dual distractions to tell the dealer he wanted to cash out.

The dealer looked helplessly at Robotov; leaving early was just not done in high-stakes games like this.

"Why are you in such a hurry, my friend?" Robotov asked Friendly.

Friendly shrugged. "I have to catch a flight."

That's all he said.

Robotov gave the dealer a curt nod and the man counted out Friendly's winnings. Friendly gave the dealer a $100,000 tip, and then gathered up his cash. Though it was mostly hundred dollar bills, there were still lots of them—way too many for the complimentary briefcase. No matter. Friendly took two elegant-looking draw-string trash bags off one of the food carts, stuffed his winnings inside them and then walked out just as the room service people were unveiling the food.

It was exactly midnight.

Robotov looked at two of his biggest bodyguards. No words were needed.

Both men hurried out of the room and were soon on Friendly's tail.

Chapter Two

It was a cold and foggy morning in San Diego.

Chris Starr took one look out the bedroom window, noted the unusual springtime weather and rolled back over on the bed.

"No sun, no fun . . ." he thought aloud.

His cell rang a moment later. Sleepily picking up the old flip phone, he saw the words: "Research Department, Suitland, Maryland."

He sat straight up in the bed.

The call was coming from the center of operations for ONI—the Office of U.S. Naval Intelligence. Starr's boss, Admiral TJ Hawley, was on the line, waiting to talk to him directly. This didn't happen too often.

It was a brief conversation. Starr had a new case: a fugitive was on the run somewhere in Ireland with ten million dollars in cash. British Intelligence was certain the money was headed for a new version of the Irish Republican Army called the Ultra-IRA or UIRA. Obsessively secret and particularly violent, the upstart UIRA had already been declared a terrorist organization by both the United States and Great Britain.

Starr's job was to find the fugitive before he made contact with the terrorists. Other pertinent details would be texted to him.

As with all his cases, the mission was deeply classified.

Starr was twenty-five, stood five foot nine, was blond, handsome and trim. On graduating from the U.S. Naval Academy, he'd dreamed of flying jets off aircraft carriers. But when a Navy psych test showed he possessed about 30-percent more ESP ability than the average person, he was made a special investigator instead and assigned to NILE, Naval Intelligence Law Enforcement. A little-known division of the ONI, NILE caught cases that were either too weird or too classified for the Navy's regular NCIS agents. He'd been at it for almost three years, working out of the U.S. Navy's vast San Diego shipyard.

Starr had an unusual type of ESP called STPA2—for short-term partially advanced precognitive ability. He didn't see things in the far future; he usually saw things just a second or two before they happened, in Navy vernacular: "pre-cog shrinkage."

He knew when a bad guy was going to throw a punch, but only in enough time to duck. Yet being two seconds ahead of the game could make a big difference when chasing bad guys, weapons ablaze at 120 MPH Either way, it was an odd ability to have.

It was always best not to ask too many questions of the Admiral, but Starr needed to know one thing. Chasing a bagman for a *noveau*-IRA around Ireland didn't seem to be a U.S. Navy problem or even an American one.

So he asked: "How do we figure into this, sir?"

The reply was blunt.

"The fugitive used to be attached to SEAL Team Six," the Admiral told him. "He's one of ours—so we've got to go get him."

Starr lived with his cover-model girlfriend, Angel.

Sort of . . .

He occupied an apartment on the top floor of The Park 12 on Imperial Avenue, close to the Navy base. Angel lived next door. Because neither of their employers would be happy with a cohabitation arrangement, Starr had built a secret passageway between his unit and Angel's. They called it the wormhole.

Angel was showering, getting ready for a photo shoot in LA, when he got the call from the Admiral. By the time he passed through the wormhole, cleaned up, packed a bag and returned to the other side, she was ready to go. Her limo had just pulled up outside.

They met in her living room; she was just brushing out her hair. Angel was stunning. Strawberry blonde hair, killer body, killer smile. It was no surprise she sometimes made more in a day than Starr did in a year. But they were both 25, in love and planning to marry one day soon.

He was in a hurry, too; his flight east left in less than thirty minutes. But he had to stop for a moment to look at her. She was dressed in a short, dark-blue skirt and matching jacket, black heels and a pair of huge, Clark-Kent eyeglasses.

"Politician's hot wife?" he guessed.

"Sexy librarian," she sweetly corrected him. "Cover shot for *Cosmo LA*. They're doing a special issue on literacy."

"You're kidding . . ."

She gave him the look. "Not everyone buys it just for the pictures."

She spotted his packed bag. "Can you give me a hint where you are going?"

Starr checked to make sure his service pistol was loaded and on safety. Everything NILE did took place deep inside the world of black ops. But Angel had a way of wiggling it out of him.

"Let's just say we're getting some of their crappy weather today," he finally replied.

***

They left together, kissing in the elevator the whole way down. The doors opened to reveal her stretch waiting outside in the fog and rain.

She stopped, held both his hands and looked into his eyes.

This was the ritual.

"I love you, Chris," she said, "So please, for me, be careful . . ."

Starr promised he would, then looked her up and down one more time.

"Is there any way you can keep that outfit, you know, for later?" he asked sheepishly.

She kissed him again and said: "I'll ask . . ."

Then she climbed into the limo and was gone.

Chapter Three

Nine hours later
Outside Cork, Ireland

The taxi skidded to a stop in front of the ancient moss-covered stone building.

Starr hastily unbuckled his seatbelt and fell out of the cab. He was dizzy and his stomach was doing flips. He'd been on some wild rides in his career—in cars, trucks, in crashing airplanes—but nothing like this.

He'd hailed the cab at Cork Airport, the last step in his transit from the other side of the world. His bosses at NILE were famous for getting their agents where they had to be very quickly, and this time was no exception. Leaving San Diego and arriving at nearby Miramar Naval Air Station, Starr was first loaded onto an F-15FXL fighter plane. The super-fast, long-range test variant of the famous F-15 Eagle traversed the country at high speed. Landing at Pease Air Force Base in New Hampshire, Starr transferred to a CIA-contracted Gulfstream G-600 which carried him across the Atlantic, again at very high speed.

Once down, all that remained was getting to his IP in the village of White's Cross, twenty miles outside Cork. A simple cab ride—or so he thought. Instead he'd endured a twisting, gyrating journey through the Irish countryside, his shaved-head, heavily-tatted driver rarely looking at the road, lest it take away from the details of his many successes at the famous Killarney Racetrack. All this while speaking in a thick brogue and going full buster—on the opposite side of the road.

Somehow, Starr made it alive.

He paid his horse-happy pal, and the cab departed in a spray of gravel and exhaust, leaving Starr alone with his hastily packed gig bag. It was 10 p.m. and chilly, but the sky overhead was clear, and the stars were out.

The building before him was Glenballey Castle. High walls, drawbridge, tower, the works. The bottom floor housed a tavern called "The Bull & Chain." A small sign over the front door identified it as "Eire's Most Haunted Pub."

Starr walked in to find it dark, but lively. Very old, very Irish, pipe music was playing in the background. He was here to meet an agent from the Special Detective Unit, Ireland's primary anti-terrorist squad. Starr's file had been sent to the SDU earlier; their agent would recognize him and make first contact.

He scanned the bar. About a dozen men were either seated or standing on the rail, all middle aged. Pints of beer and whiskey glasses abounded. Starr was a good part Irish, so none of this surprised him. But maybe his contact was just hiding under a good cover.

A young girl approached in the dim light; Starr ID'd her as one of the wait staff.

"I'm sorry," he told her. "I don't need a table. I'm just looking for a friend."

"And I'm that friend," she replied in a pleasant lilt.

Starr snapped to and took a better look at her.

She was in her mid-20s, five-foot-four, not quite petite, with dark red hair and incredibly bright blue eyes— they looked almost neon. She was wearing a green buttoned-up sweater, a short green tartan skirt, black tights and clogs.

And she was looking up at him very sweetly with a gigantic smile.

Starr started to apologize, but she was already shaking her head.

"Don't worry," she said, slyly displaying her SDU badge. "Special Agent Maura McCann. And it happens all the time."

She led him to a dark corner booth.

Her overnight bag was so enormous, it was taking up the entire bench on one side. So they sat together on the other side, she letting him in first and then squeezing in after him.

Politely waving off a waitress, she took out her tablet and began reading the case notes.

"Our mark's name is Fred Friendly," she said. "Curious fellow. Won ten million dollars off some hoodlums in a card game in Boston. Next spotted at Boston's Logan Airport. Security cameras see him going into a rest room around three a.m., followed by two known button men from a local Russian Mob.

"Two minutes later, Friendly emerges from the rest room alone and intact. He's still carrying what's believed to be the money in two large ornate garbage bags. When a cleaning crew goes into the rest room approximately ten minutes later, they find the two hitmen dead. Each by a single kick to the laryngeal prominence."

Starr grimaced. "Crushed larynx. Nasty . . ."

"It gets better," she went on. "The bodies were stretched out on the floor with drops of oil on their hands, feet and foreheads."

Starr had to think a moment. "They were given the Last Rites? Really?"

Maura nodded. "Even had salt on their tongues. Now, that's old school."

Starr was puzzled. "Friendly was attached to SEAL Team Six," he said. "I'm sure that's where he learned to kick like that. But what's with the Last Rites?"

She showed him a picture on her tablet. It was Fred Friendly wearing a combat uniform—and a priest's collar. "He was a *chaplain* for your Seal Team Six. Your higher-ups didn't mention that?"

Starr shook his head no.

Thanks, Admiral . . .

As reported to her by SDU…She detailed some of Friendly's peculiar activities since arriving in Ireland almost two days before. These included reserving a dozen rental cars and more than two dozen rooms in hotels, B&Bs and lodges in ten different parts of the country—and those were just the ones they were aware of.

"Not sure what that's about," she told him. "Unless he suspects someone is . . ."

But Starr had stopped paying attention. Maura had casually unbuttoned her sweater to reveal a white silk blouse underneath with a surprisingly plunging neckline. She was also wearing a gold necklace with a dangling crucifix. At the moment, Jesus's bouncing feet were getting lost in her demure cleavage.

He tried not to stare, but it was dawning on him that Maura was gorgeous in an unusual way. His girlfriend, Angel, was beautiful—and you knew it the moment you saw her. With Maura, it took a little while for the combination of her features to sink in.

But when they did . . .

"I made this our IP because Father Friendly was spotted here just a couple hours ago," she went on, her accent only accentuating her Hibernian sensuality. "He hung around a little bit, like he was waiting for someone. Then he asked where the nearest fueling station was and left.

"Now, British Intelligence is certain he's heading up to Belfast to hook up with the UIRA. But my DHQ thinks with all the false hotel reservations he made, he might actually be staying on this side of the border for the night, maybe even somewhere close by."

"MI-6 isn't infallible," Starr replied with a shrug. "He could be doing the money transfer down here, in this part of Ireland."

"I agree," she said. "And it wouldn't be the first time the Brit spooks were wrong."

Maura was brimming with enthusiasm for the case, but Starr was still distracted. She was sitting very close to him and he'd noticed she was wearing an unusual piece of jewelry in her right ear. It was an angel with two tiny blinking emerald lights on its wings. Her left lobe was earring-free.

Starr found this oddly suggestive. Doesn't the right ear mean something? he thought.

"So, what do you think so far?" she asked, once again knocking him back to reality.

"Do we know what kind of car he's actually driving?"

She checked her tablet. "Although he made those dozen rental reservations, in Killarney, Donegal, Dublin—all over—he's only followed through on one of them so far. It's from a specialty car-leasing service in Cork. A 1966 Jaguar E-Type Special-12 . . ."

Starr laughed. "You're kidding, right?"

"I don't think so," she replied. "Why?"

"That model Jaguar is considered the worst Jaguar ever built," he said. "The engine blows smoke, the transmission burns fluid. Everything on it leaks and its exhaust smells really, really bad. There can't be more than fifty of them in the world still in driving condition."

"Not a good getaway car then?"

"I guess it depends on how far you want to go," he said. "It gets about five miles a gallon at best. So no matter where he's headed, he'll need to stop for gas along the way, and . . ."

"And if we can find out where he's 'gassing up,'" she finished his thought for him. ". . . we could get a hot tail on him pretty quickly."

She stopped talking for a moment and looked him up and down.

"I know a bit about you, you know," she said, surprising him.

"You do?"

She nodded slowly, comically squinting as if studying him through a virtual magnifying glass.

"The San Diego Dick-Chick Case?" she began. "Marine hero murders his transvestite girlfriend; you break the case. Then some old guy builds a tank and starts bombarding a little town near Boston—on Christmas Eve, in a super-blizzard . . . and you break the case. Someone is using WMD in the African jungle; *you* break the case. It was all in the dossier your bosses sent over. Lots of commendations. Very impressive . . ."

"They write those things to sound dramatic," he told her.

She reached over and tapped his hand twice. "That's because they *are* dramatic," she replied.

He was about to say: Well, tell me about yourself . . . when she got an alert of some kind. A buzzing, a beeping, he couldn't tell which. She gathered up her dangling necklace, slipped out of the booth and wandered into the darkest part of the pub. Starr innocently tried to catch her side of the conversation, but couldn't.

Thirty seconds later, she was back—and buttoning up her sweater.

"My DHQ says Friendly just paid a toll on the M20 motorway not far from here," she reported. "He's driving north, but he's heading towards Limerick—not the most direct route if he's going to Belfast. The Queen's spooks might indeed be wrong again."

Starr had started helping her with her gear, but then stopped for a moment.

"Limerick?" he said. "Isn't that the place they call 'Stab City'?"

She jabbed him in the ribs. "I'll protect you," she said, grabbing her enormous overnight bag. "Now, let's go . . ."

Maura nodded to the bartender as they walked out; the man nodded back. Starr zipped up his jacket, put on his cap and opened the pub's front door for her . . . to find a wall of thick fog waiting on the other side.

He couldn't see two feet in front of him.

"What the fa . . .?" he cried. "It was clear as hell when I got here five minutes ago. How can anything change so quickly?"

She took his arm and led him to her car.

"Welcome to Ireland," she said.

Chapter Four

Two minutes later, Starr's heart was pounding louder than at any time during his taxi ride from hell earlier.

While the cabbie had been a distracted driver, Maura just seemed crazy behind the wheel. Her vehicle was a basic 2016 Volvo V-90 and it was every bit a cop car, down to the smell of spilled coffee and cigarette smoke, to the shotgun holsters built into the side panels of the front doors.

But it didn't have fog lamps—and the four-lane M20 motorway was seriously socked in. The visibility was down to inches beyond the hood, wipers clacking in constant motion to clear the windshield of mist. The M20 also had plenty of curves. But Maura was taking every bend and turn with no fear, headlights on low beam, pushing 110 kilometers an hour, almost 70 MPH in Starr's world.

It was about thirty miles to Limerick, and no big surprise, no one else was on the road. Still, Starr wondered if he could just close his eyes and wait for it to be over, one way or another.

But something very odd interrupted that plan.

They were about ten miles up the M20 when they came to a steep hill. Below was a tiny hamlet called

Ballypens where the highway intersected with two state roads. A pair of flashing traffic lights was barely visible in thick mist. Yet Maura stayed right on the gas.

Down the hill at high speed and about fifty yards out, Starr would remember seeing two things: the glint of a security camera atop one of the traffic lights and a small Benz delivery truck parked at the side of the road.

That's when his STPA2 suddenly kicked in.

Something bad, straight ahead . . .

He went to reach for the car's emergency brake . . . but a split second before he could act, Maura beat him to it. She pulled up on the hand brake, while calmly pumping the foot brakes and turning hard to the left. Physics took over, spinning the car to a violent stop, just inches before the intersection.

The Benz delivery van blew up a moment later. There was a bright, muffled explosion, lighting up the mist with a sick orange glow. Then a cascade of truck parts and debris began falling out of the dark, foggy night.

Ten more feet into the intersection and they'd have both been killed.

Without missing a beat, Maura turned the nose of the Volvo back in the right direction, hit the accelerator and roared past the burning truck.

"That was an IED," she said, excited but in control. "Someone was trying to kill us. Do you agree?"

"One hundred percent," Starr replied.

"Then you mind if I don't stop?"

"Not at all . . ."

That's all she needed to hear. She buried the accelerator now and they were quickly speeding back down the murky highway, the speedometer needle climbing until it passed from Starr's view.

He was all for leaving the scene because these things sometimes came in twos. But there was an even bigger question on his mind. Maura had saved their lives back there, not only because, he now realized, she obviously knew tactical driving, but also because she'd acted not at the precise moment needed—but actually a couple seconds before it. Like she knew what was going to happen just moments before it actually did happen. That was the textbook definition of STPA2—short-term partially advanced precognitive ability. Starr's rare brand of ESP.

"How did you do that?" he asked her.

She knew what he was talking about. But she shrugged self-consciously, eyes straight ahead, the cross on her necklace jingling as it bounced against her chest.

"If I told you I have a guardian angel," she replied. "Could we just leave it at that?"

Chapter Five

They arrived in Limerick just after midnight.

The fog had worsened, and the road became even more winding the farther north they'd driven. But the journey had taken on a new vibe. Starr had worked with CIA evasion specialists who couldn't drive half as well as Maura. ESP aside, it was her training that actually saved them.

It was the truck bomb that was on their minds now, though. Starr had had attempts on his life before—so had she—and there was an insidious terror to it. You were grateful to be alive, but concerned that someone tried to kill you.

They'd stopped at four petrol stations along the M20. None had seen the odd ball Jaguar. Aside from this, most of their conversation centered on whether Father Friendly could have engineered the murder attempt. Considering the logistics—including somehow remotely detonating the truck bomb—it seemed unlikely.

But this man of the cloth had killed two people in the last 48 hours—and he *was* a former Navy SEAL. Who knew what he was capable of?

Topic two: If it wasn't Father Friendly, then who?

Maura had run down a list of organizations the SDU had dealt with recently. Some were suspected terrorist cells, some were simply criminals. But she couldn't recall anyone trying to kill someone with a truck bomb, not inside the Irish Republic, not in the last five years anyway. In fact, that sort of thing went out when the old IRA laid down its arms in 1998.

And why would they be the targets in the first place?

They'd just crossed over the Sarsfield Bridge into Limerick when Starr reached what would have seemed to be a simple conclusion.

"If it *was* meant for us," he said. "I think it was someone who was trying to stop us from catching Father Friendly . . ."

". . . because they want to catch him first," Maura said, completing his thought once again.

Once over the bridge and into the city, she handed Starr her tablet, directing him to a map of Limerick. It was overlaid with pulsating red-warning stripes.

"Those are the neighborhoods that SDU forbids us to go into unaccompanied," she explained. "We have to have at least one other officer with us. But we'll have to break that rule tonight."

The red warning zones encompassed eighty percent of the city.

"No mystery why they call it 'Stab City'," Starr said.

"Getting stabbed might be the least of your troubles in this place," she replied. "The whole city is off. Mother forgive me—but they're all fooking weirdos here."

They spent the next hour visiting a dozen of the city's 37 patrol stations. No one they talked to had seen a smoking, leaking, stinking Jag.

Then Maura got a tip from . . . somebody.

Starr had just finished talking to the owner of petrol station number 12 when he saw Maura slip back to the Volvo, fold her hands in prayer and lean them on the steering wheel. By the time he got into the car, she had a full report: One of the many hotel reservations the priest had made was for a place in a rundown part of east Limerick called the Grog House—and there was police activity at the scene.

Maura pushed the Grog House into her GPS. They were about a mile away. She set off, siren wailing, headlights flashing, and began expertly wheeling the Volvo through the dirty, foggy streets.

They passed through some of the city's most dangerous spots: Perry Square, People's Park, Dock Road and the railway station. Even in the thick mist, Starr could see figures huddled around doorways and at the entrances to pubs, eying the Volvo as it raced by.

They were heading for O'Connell Street, home to so many seedy clubs, back alleys and dark places, the SDU security division warned its agents this particular section of Stab City "should be avoided at all costs, unless in dire emergency."

The Grog House was at 101 O'Connell Street. As shown on the tablet, it was a crumbling building in a sea of crumbling buildings, the most inhospitable hotel imaginable. Coming up on it now, they could see two police cars were parked out front, their spinning blue lights lending an eerie, syncopated glow to the fog.

Maura stopped the Volvo in a controlled skid, going right up on the curb, and they jumped out. She had her SDU badge up at eye level as they went past the police guard at the hotel's front door and into the shabby lobby. Above the registration desk was a sign: "Ireland's Most Haunted Inn."

There were a half dozen members of the local Garda inside. Maura found the highest-ranking officer and asked to be briefed. But the man was an old timer and basically shrugged her off.

"We are investigating a double homicide, Miss," he said dryly. "Two victims. Second floor, Corner room. You can have a look if you like."

He started to walk away, but Maura caught him by the arm.

"Is one of them a priest?" she asked him.

Suddenly, the cop was paying attention.

"No," he replied. "We believe they were hired guns of some sort. But they were here looking for a priest. . ."

Maura pushed past him, saying over her shoulder that the entire building was now an SDU crime scene and no one, even the local cops, could come in or go out.

The officer began flustering. "Wait—what's this all about?" he called after her—but she was already gone, through the lobby and up the stairs to the second floor.

She left behind a mouthful of choice words, followed by "Mother forgive me . . ."

The officer became very upset.

"What did she just call me?" he demanded of Starr.

Starr just shrugged.

"I think she said: 'On the whole, it's classified'. . .

Maura was interrogating the inn's owner by the time Starr reached the second floor. The man was Rumanian and couldn't speak English, but no problem, Maura was firing questions at him in Moldavian and Transylvanian. He understood both.

She translated the virtual tower of babble back to Starr in concise microbursts. "The two men inside are dead, they died with neck injuries," she said. "They had been very nervous waiting for the priest to arrive. When they saw him in the lobby, they waited a minute then followed him up to his room. The priest left a short time later, bags packed. He paid the bill in American cash. He gave a quick blessing to one of the homeless women who lives on the inn's front doorstep and then was gone."

"Why were they so nervous waiting for him to get here?" Starr asked. Maura translated and the man rattled off a torrent of words while making three hectic signs of the cross.

"This place is haunted," she said he said. "The dead men did not like being in a haunted place."

Starr and Maura looked at each other for a moment and then mouthed the same word, at the same time.

"Albanians?"

People from Albania were the most superstitious people on Earth. Albanians believed in every ghost, dark spirit, vampire, witch, and unlucky omen in the book, A to Z. Some even drank holy water in the morning to ward off any nasty stuff they might encounter during the day. As it turned out, Albanians were also known as among the best assassins in the world. Ruthless and fearless, they worked relatively cheap and so were in high demand.

Starr and Maura had both dealt with them before.

"I don't think they came to see the shamrocks," she told him.

They went into the room to find the two bodies just as reported: lying side by side between two beds, faces up, throats crushed.

There was oil on their foreheads and hands and feet, and a pinch of salt on their lips. The Last Rites again . . .

"Just can't help himself, I guess," Maura said, taking close-up pictures of the stiffs and the ceremony's components.

Starr took some of the oil from one goon's forehead, rubbed it between his fingers, then tasted it.

"He's really got problems with that car's transmission," he declared. "Not only must it be leaking, it's overheating too, and he has to keep putting fluid into it."

"You know that just from a taste?"

"And the smell," he replied. "He had it on his fingers when he gave these guys their goodbye kiss."

She took his hand, put his fingers to her nose and grimaced.

"That's a hard odor to miss," she said, gently pushing him away.

"Especially when it's been burnt," he said, sniffing it again. "Just like that DIY tank you heard about, he's going to need some kind of service soon. If not, the car might just die on him."

She had her tablet out again, but started talking even before the screen came alive.

"All the petrol stations in town are closed by now," she said.

Once again, Starr noticed she was saying the words before they could have possibly appeared on her screen. Once again, she seemed to be two steps ahead. The strangest thing was he knew *something* was happening because it would take a person who had STPA2, or something close to it, to recognize it in another.

"So he probably won't gas up here," Starr said, switching gears. "Not unless he wants to hang around until morning. Though, after adding to his body count here, I'd say that's unlikely."

Maura started patting down the dead men. The first stiff was clean. But when she reached into the second man's jacket pocket, she came out with a receipt.

"Rental slip for a Benz delivery van, written two miles from White's Cross," she said, her hand to her lips. "Oh my God . . ."

"Well, now we know who was trying to kill us," Starr told her, taking the receipt. "And prevent us from getting here."

But Maura was already gone.

Chapter Six

She was belted in by the time Starr reached the Volvo.

Leaning on the steering wheel, her hands were folded as if in prayer, her crucifix and chain interlocked between her fingers.

Starr didn't want to barge in on her private moment. But she'd seen him approaching and waved him into the car.

She was upset, fighting her emotions.

"Everything OK?" he asked.

"Those two goons," she said, letting the crucifix go but still staring straight ahead. "They must have been sent by that Russian mobster, trying to get his ten million back, right?"

"Yes, makes sense . . ."

"And they're the guys who tried to kill us," she went on. "But how in hell did they know we were even involved? They must have made us at the Bull & Chain and called someone. There's no other way. And that's my fault for suggesting we meet there. Such a rookie mistake. I almost got us killed . . ."

But Starr just waved her concerns away.

"First of all, you saved our lives from getting greased by that truck bomb," he told her. "And second, those humps were chasing Father Friendly just like we are. So we were going to run into them at some point anyway. And you were right before. They tried to kill us so they could get to Friendly before we did. But he solved that problem for us. So no harm, no foul. Don't worry about it."

She looked over at him, a glimmer of light returning to her eyes. He thought she was going to hug him. And he was going to let her. But after a few moments slipped by, she started the car, turned on the headlights and adjusted her mirrors. She was back to all business.

"Judging from the condition of those stiffs," he said to her, "we're probably less than an hour behind him. But where to?"

"He's got a thing about haunted houses," she replied. "The Bull and Chain, and now this place. And it sure helped him here. I think he knew those Albanian mooks were coming after him, and he got them nervous *before* he kicked their throats in."

She turned her map app on. "My DHQ says there's a village about twenty miles from here called Shawnsbridge. It's off the M23. They have a BNB that claims to have a haunted statue of Saint Patrick. Its eyes move when no one's looking. Other than that, nothing haunted for another hundred or so miles."

"Does this place have a filling station?" Starr asked.

"There's a petrol station at the north end of town, near the highway. But it's closed until 0600 tomorrow."

Starr checked his watch. It was almost 1 a.m.

"If he's headed for Shawnsbridge and he's low on fuel, he'll have no choice but to wait until six before gassing up again. And he's going to need some transmission fluid really soon too. Unless he's carrying extra quarts of the stuff, that's got to be priority 1A for him."

Her face brightened.

"Boy, if we could ever jump him before six tomorrow morning . . ." she said.

". . . then we could put a bow on this one by breakfast," he finished for her.

She threw the car in gear and buried the accelerator. The Volvo rocketed down O'Connell Street and disappeared into the mist.

Chapter Seven

They checked three filling stations along the M23 motorway before reaching Shawnsbridge.

All three were already closed for the night. Studying their aprons and the ground around their fuel pumps, Starr found no trace of the burnt transmission fluid that Father Friendly's car was probably trailing behind it.

This due diligence and the unrelenting fog made the trip to Shawnsbridge twice as long as it should have been. It was almost 3 a.m. by the time they pulled into the tiny village.

It looked like a travel poster for the Old Sod. Small, rustic, authentic, lots of fields, mountains in the background. The miniature triangular town center was bordered by a tavern, a youth hostel and the haunted BNB, which was called The Cross & Bottle Inn. An alley next to the BNB led to a rear lot where they could see a red 1966 Jaguar-E parked under a streetlight, a small pool of transmission fluid glistening beneath it in the misty sodium glow.

Maura was cool. She drove right by the place with practiced nonchalance, but doing so with only one hand. She had her tablet out and was madly typing with the other, sending a message to someone, requesting the go-ahead to apprehend the suspect.

"Got eyes on the mark's vehicle," she recited as she typed. "We'll be able to get in position and arrest him in about five minutes."

But then . . . nothing. They waited fifteen minutes, twenty; parked at the far end of the village, it seemed like an eternity.

"This is not good," Maura said, over and over. Starr agreed with her: Delays in execution orders usually meant someone up top was thinking too deeply, not always a good thing.

So when her response finally arrived, it didn't surprise them.

But it was infuriating.

"This is coming directly from SDU Central in Dublin—not my DHQ," she said, seething. "Their instructions are to delay taking Friendly into custody until 0900—nine in the morning. They want to see if he makes contact with anyone else SDU might be interested in. So, this is now a damn surveillance mission."

"They're rolling the dice," Starr told her, feeling her frustration. "Once you've got a big fish hooked, you never know who's going to jump in the boat with him. But a lot of times, it doesn't work out that way."

She threw the tablet into the back seat.

"They want us to go code sixty-two until 0900," she said.

"Code sixty-two? What's that mean?"

She looked over at him, annoyed, angry but still smiling.

"It means you and I are going to shack up together..."

They roused the owners of the youth hostel and Maura told them the situation. The place was empty of lodgers this time of year, which was good. The owners promised to cooperate in any way needed.

Meanwhile, Maura received news from her DHQ that the priest had taken a room on the second floor of the haunted BNB. With this in mind, they were able to set up in a small dormitory directly across the street from the priest's rented room.

Starr opened his gig bag, broke out his night vision goggles and activated their Super Ears app. "Can you take the first shift?" Maura asked him, unzipping her own, much larger, overnight bag. "I'd love a nap."

"Good plan," he answered. "Good to stay sharp . . ."

She smiled at him though in a quizzical way. "Always," she said.

She slipped into the bathroom, bag in hand. He heard the shower turn on.

He took up a position in the room's small bay window and clicked on the night vision goggles. They were ENVG-Bs, the most advanced design in NV; this would be the first time he'd used them. It was still extremely foggy outside, yet the new goggles easily cut through the dark and mist, making it, to his eyes, almost a bright, sunny day. The clarity was astonishing. Plus, the Super Ears app allowed him to hear a directed target as far as a mile away.

He settled in, his new electronically enhanced eyes focused on the old stone building across the street, 25 feet away. There were two windows in the priest's room; the curtains were open, but the place was dark. Starr directed the Super Ears to concentrate on the room, but all was quiet inside as well.

Only in the movies were stakeouts shown to be cool. In truth, like any kind of peeping-tom activity, there was usually lots of downtime.

Ten minutes went by; Starr heard the shower turn off. A minute after that, the door opened and Maura re-emerged. Without thinking, he turned to look at her—and felt like he'd been hit by a bolt of lightning.

She'd changed into a very thin, very tiny, very short nightgown. A baby doll, they used to call them. And thanks to his new NVGs, and their cutting-edge light and heat equalizer, he could see right through it.

London, France and everything in between, Maura was stunning, top to bottom, inside and out.

He hastily banged off the NVGs, electronically averting his eyes and knocking himself back to the real world. Looking more like a shadow now, she glided across the room, reached the large four-poster bed—and went down on her knees.

Her hair now wrapped in a towel, she took up her chain and once again held it tightly between her fingers. Putting the crucifix to her lips, she began whispering.

And this time, Starr could hear everything she was saying.

He'd extinguished his porno-vision, but the Super Ears app was still engaged. He hastily shut it off too, but not before catching a snippet of Maura's voice.

She was not praying. She was one side of a two-part conversation. Like on a phone call, Maura was talking directly to someone.

Strange . . .

Starr was Irish, but he hadn't spent much time in Ireland.

Did people talk directly to their guardian angels here?

He reactivated the NVGs and the Super Ears, then turned back towards Father Friendly's room.

Suddenly he felt a tap on his shoulder. He swung around and *again* he was looking at an infrared image of see-through Maura. And now she was standing right next to him, her hand resting lightly on his shoulder.

"Can you wake me in a while then?" she asked, smiling at him in the ethereal glow of NightVision. She looked like an actress from a soft-core movie.

"For sure," he coughed in reply.

She said thanks, padded away and climbed into the bed. She was snoring softly thirty seconds later.

But Starr was still shaken, and would be long afterwards.

Who brings a negligee to a stakeout?

Chapter Eight

The clock in the village's tiny church had just struck six when the Range Rover pulled up in front of the haunted BNB.

Starr immediately locked on to the vehicle with his NVGs and turned the Super Ears to full directional. Two men climbed out of the dark green truck, took a careful look around the deserted town center, then retrieved two suitcases and went through the BNB's front door.

There was no need to check the NILE criminal database for these two—Starr knew they were bad guys, whoever they were. He had to admit SDU Dublin Central's decision to roll the dice was looking better.

Starr followed the pair's progress, window by window, through the BNB. A quick stop at the deserted registration desk to look at the guest book, then up the stairs to the second floor and finally to the priest's room. The lights came on as soon as they opened his door.

Starr slipped out of his spot in the bay window and quietly made his way to the bed to wake Maura.

But, then suddenly . . .

Protect her . . .

The bomb went off a moment later.

The blast was so powerful it ripped a hole in the side of the BNB *and* blew away the hostel's bay window where Starr had just been sitting. A storm of hot glass and burning splinters tore through the room—then the hostel's roof caved in, two heavy wooden beams crashing down on top of the four-poster bed.

But Starr and Maura were unhurt. He'd followed his pre-cog voice and had fallen on top of her in that instant before the blast went off. Then, all in one motion, he'd rolled her up in the blankets and they fell to the floor together, just before the beams came down. A second bomb went off a moment later, once again sending a blizzard of sizzling glass shards through the dorm room. But they stayed on the floor and remained unscathed.

It took a few long seconds before everything stopped shaking. Then came an eerie quiet. Nothing but the wind and the crackle of flames coming from the haunted BNB.

Starr had his .357 out—pure reflex. And as they disentangled themselves from the blankets and debris, he saw that Maura, wide awake and alert, was also armed. She'd been sleeping with a SIG P365 pistol.

"The priest's room?" she asked as they scrambled around the rubble.

"Blown to bits, I'm sure," Starr replied, yelling over the wind. They could hear emergency units already approaching in the distance. "We've got to get down there quick."

She was way ahead of him. Throwing on a long sweater and shoes, she went out the door, pistol at the ready. Starr was close behind.

They found the hostel's proprietor and his wife stumbling out the front door. They were dazed but unharmed. Maura told them to go to the church nearby, break in if they had to, and shelter in place.

Then she and Starr went across the street. The Range Rover was totally involved in flames by now; so was the tavern next door. The few other guests in the BNB came staggering out of the doorway, collapsing into the street, some injured seriously.

The village's EMTs arrived and began attending the injured. The fire brigade roared down the street seconds later. Townspeople were starting to appear as well, some carrying fire extinguishers and even buckets of water and garden hoses.

"Two nail bombs," Maura told Starr, looking at the damage to the outside of the BNB. "Lots of shrapnel. Someone wanted to get a job done right."

"We've got to get inside," he told her. "See what's what . . ."

Maura flashed her SDU badge to the commander of the fire brigade and told him they had to enter the damaged building as it was a crime scene. The man did not try to stop her, but begged her to be careful.

She and Starr entered the BNB's lobby. It was dark and filled with smoke. Two broken pipes were spraying water everywhere. There was so much debris it took five minutes just to reach the stairway. Getting up to the second floor was just as difficult as its ceiling had collapsed, forcing them to go one step at a time.

There was another wall of debris at the top of the landing, but at least from here they were able to look into what had been the priest's room. The inner walls had all been blown out, so they had a full view.

Two bodies were lying on the other side of the room's doorway. They'd been perforated by thousands of nails and were soaked in blood. But Starr and Maura could still see splotches of oil glimmering on the hands, feet and foreheads, and white salt crystals stuck to their lips, signs of the Last Rites.

They were astonished. These were the bad guys.

The priest had escaped again.

"I don't believe this," Maura said. "Who the hell is he?"

"He might be a magician," Starr said surveying the damage and detecting the patterns of the shrapnel spray. "Because I think these guys got killed by their own bombs before they were able to plant them outside his room. And if his body isn't a puddle of goo in there somewhere, that means he survived the blast, gave these two mooks Extreme Unction and *then* made his escape."

A quick look through a hole in the side of the building and into the parking lot out back confirmed it: the Jag was gone.

"I knew your SEAL Team Six guys were good," Maura moaned. "But this is crazy . . ."

"But how the hell did he do it?" Starr wondered looking around the devastated room. "And where is he now?"

Just then they heard a tremendous roar—it rivaled the sound of the police and firefighters' klaxons. They made their way to the edge of the devastated room and looked down on the foggy, rubble-strewn street below—just in time to see Father Friendly's bright red Jaguar go rocketing by, engine roaring, leaving behind a tailwind of blowing fog and disappearing into the night.

"My God," Maura exclaimed. "These bombs went off more than ten minutes ago. Why did he wait so long to make his getaway?"

Starr looked at his watch. It was 6:20 in the morning. He just shook his head wearily.

"Because he stopped to get the gas . . ." he said.

Chapter Nine

They left Shawnsbridge twenty minutes later.

It was a tough call. Half the village was on fire and the flames were spreading. All the local emergency services were on hand, but whether they could handle the situation looked iffy at best. More help was enroute, but at least ten minutes away.

Still, Starr and Maura set off after Father Friendly, but the decision didn't come lightly. Both felt at least partly responsible for bringing hell down on the tiny hamlet, just a couple killer angels passing through. But they had to get on with the job.

The roll of the dice by Dublin Central had born some unusual fruit. The idea that other bad guys—whoever they were—would try to make contact with Friendly had been right on the money. But while the world had two less goons to worry about, Shawnsbridge was burning down, the bad guys were dust and their mark had gotten away.

Starr did the math. Now with a full tank of gas in Shawnsbridge, and by taking the most direct route to Ulster County, the Jag could reach the border in about three hours, Belfast less than an hour after that. And while the foggy conditions would hinder him as much as them, the priest had at least a thirty-minute head-start.

This was now a chase. While SDU vowed to ramp-up all of its air and ground assets and have them looking for Friendly by morning, Starr and Maura knew wrangling combined resources like that always took longer than anticipated. By that time, it would be too late.

So, in the last few hours of this long night, it seemed only they had any chance of catching the fugitive priest.

Five minutes up the M23, they reached a place called Holy Home Farms.

About a quarter mile ahead they could see two Garda cars, blue lights spinning, blocking the highway. Two policemen in yellow fluorescent jackets were manning the detour. They were madly waving their flashlights at the oncoming Volvo.

Maura pulled up to them, holding her SDU badge out the window. They explained the next twelve miles of the road had been closed due to so many car accidents in the thick fog. Because she was SDU, they could let her through, but they estimated it would take at least an hour to get around the wrecks and all the emergency equipment.

The alternate route would put them on secondary roads for about fifteen miles, at which point they could get back onto the M23 and continue north towards Ulster. This would burn time they couldn't afford, but there seemed no other option.

"By the way, have you seen a red Jaguar tonight?" Maura asked the cops.

"The priest?" one replied. "He was here about fifteen minutes ago. Nice car, but smelly."

Fifteen minutes . . .

They were closer to Friendly than they thought.

Re-energized, Maura slammed the Volvo back in gear.

"That's good to know," she told the policemen. "We've been trying to catch up with him."

She began wheeling the car towards the detour, but suddenly stopped—it was just long enough to hear the second cop say: "But you won't catch him if you go that way."

Maura went in reverse for a few feet, back to where the cops were standing.

Both men were pointing to their right. "He's heading that way, Miss," one said. "Towards Galway . . ."

But this didn't make sense. Galway was to the northwest, and off any straight route to Ulster.

"Are you sure it's Galway?" Starr asked, leaning over Maura.

"He asked us for the directions . . ." was the cop's reply. "We sent him to the N59 . . ."

Thirty minutes later, they were traveling on route N59, a two-lane highway that ran along the rocky coast of Galway.

In one way it was similar to the other roadways they'd faced tonight—lots of hills and unexpected dips. But the closer they got to the coast, the more sharp curves and high cliffs they encountered. Starr was sure that in clear daylight, N59 would be perfect for a travelogue. But in the dark and the unrelenting mist, the unlit road was treacherous.

Still there was no bend too sharp, hill too steep or fog bank too thick, to prevent Maura from traveling at 110/k/h.

She talked non-stop—but Starr enjoyed it. Strategy, tactics, that any good investigator knew it was wise to expect the unexpected. But this latest twist had them both baffled. Why was Father Friendly driving through Galway? He'd made no hotel and car rental reservations in that part of Ireland, at least that they knew of. And the UIRA had no known presence there.

But, if as British Intelligence thought, Belfast was the priest's destination, he sure was taking the long way around.

***

Hearkening back to the time he tracked the Abrams DIY tank up and down a barrier island off Massachusetts, he asked Maura to stop about fifteen miles into Galway, just as they reached the coast. Using his NVGs, he was able to see the heat signature of a stream of the hot liquid that had been dropped on the pavement not too long before. Taking a bit on his finger and holding it to his nose, it was unmistakable. The smelly '66 Jag had passed here no more than ten minutes ago.

They were catching up to him.

Twenty minutes later, they stopped again, this time at the peak of a hill that looked out over some enormous and ominous rock formations with the roaring North Atlantic beyond.

He found more evidence the Jag had been here recently, but more importantly, the "hot dots" of the smelly substance were fewer and far between. Father Friendly was running out of tranny fluid.

When they stopped once again ten miles later, Starr didn't even need to get out of the car. He just put this nose out the window and took a sniff. That distinctive odor of an '66 Jag-E Special 12 was as thick in the night air as the mist.

Starr estimated the priest was about five miles in front of them, no more.

Driving along even faster than before, the conversation took an unexpected turn when Maura suddenly slipped into in a famous Irish pastime: the guilt trip.

Luckily, Starr remembered these things from family get-togethers in his youth. He knew better than to interrupt.

"I thought I had my head screwed on straight," she'd moaned. "From the day I graduated the academy, I promised myself I wouldn't make stupid rookie mistakes. But now look at me . . .

"Picking the Bull & Chain as our meeting place? Rookie mistake. Getting emotional after finding that receipt? Rookie mistake. Not telling Dublin Central to go fook themselves, that we had to take down this guy immediately—because he was both a SEAL and a slippery character—but I didn't. Rookie mistake! And now we're driving through Galway for God's sake . . ."

It took about five kilometers for her to lay out a litany of her sins and self-diagnosed stupidity. Then she took a deep breath and got quiet. Eyes straight ahead, roaring along, it was not the natural state of affairs for her.

Starr let another minute go by. Only then did he speak.

"It's never a bad thing to dissect your mistakes," he told her calmly. "How else are we going to learn? But it's not a good thing to beat yourself up over them either. Besides, what you think of as screw-ups, I just think are the typical bumps in the road, things that always happen during jobs like this. So, we should just . . ."

He never got out the rest of the sentence. Maura suddenly stood on the brakes, brought the Volvo to a screeching stop in the middle of the dark, foggy road and this time, *did* hug him. It was quick, over before he even knew what hit him. But it was very sweet and warm.

Then she composed herself, put the car in gear and they were off once again.

But not before she laughed nervously and said, "Now *that* was a rookie mistake."

Chapter Ten

Another half hour in, just beyond Killary Harbor, they crested a hill to find a serious car accident just below them.

They thought for sure that the Jag had been involved, but that was not the case. A Volkswagen Golf was burning fiercely in a field to the right. An overturned Honda pickup lay flattened in the mud of an irrigation ditch to the left. It too was blazing away.

Maura rolled up to the crash scene. Two men were sitting on the side of the road, nearly hidden in the smoke, both with seriously bloody noses.

Weapons ready, but hidden, Starr and Maura got out of their car and checked the surroundings.

Starr caught her by the arm and said: "Take a sniff..."

"Eewww," she wailed, on cue. "He was here . . ."

They approached the two men. Their vehicle was the Honda burning down in the ditch.

Up close, they saw both were also bruised and burned. Yet they were conscious enough to be sharing a flask.

Starr and Maura had the same question: how did the two men get out of the burning wreck?

Maura asked them what happened.

"He pulled us out," they both said at once.

But there was no one else about.

"Who did?" Starr asked.

Suddenly both men came out of their stupors and started paying attention.

"Hey," one of them cried, looking around. "Where's the priest? And where's the guy who was in the other car?"

The emergency room was in chaos.

Galway Memorial Hospital was located near the village of Overmoore Bridge, close to the border of County Mayo. It was run by the Sisters of Divine Mercy, an order of nuns whose Irish roots went back more than a thousand years.

The foggy conditions had caused such a cluster of car accidents in the area, the hospital staff was performing triage in the waiting room. The injured were lying on tables, on couches, on the floor. It looked like a battle ward.

Starr and Maura navigated their way around the victims and, in the middle of it all, found the head nurse, a very slight, stern-looking nun named Sister George. She looked like an Irish Mother Theresa. She was applying plastic ID bracelets to the wrists of the injured.

Maura showed her SDU credentials and asked: "Has anyone dropped off a car accident victim here in the last half hour?"

Sister George managed to look both annoyed and bemused.

"Half these people were dropped off here," she said. "The other half got here on their own. We don't have time to pay attention to how they arrived . . ."

"But this man would have been brought in by a priest, an American," Starr insisted. "Someone in his late fifties?'

The nun almost shook her head—but then stopped. Her craggy face suddenly brightened.

"He wasn't in a Roman collar," she said. "But a very generous, kind-hearted American man was here just a little while ago."

"Generous how?" Maura asked her.

"He came in with an accident victim," the nun recounted. "Adult male. Ambulatory. He's in the burn room right now, his injuries are extensive. But this Good Samaritan had treated them with mud before bringing him here and stabilized him. He must have known what he was doing. A military combat medic or something."

"But why did you say he was generous?" Starr pressed her.

"The man he brought in didn't have an insurance card," Sister George replied. "So I followed his Good Samaritan out to the parking lot to see if he had it. He was driving some kind of race car.

"I explained the situation to him—and without a word he reached into a big white bag, took out five thousand cash, U.S., and told me to pay for the man's expenses with it and give the rest to charity. Then he thanked me and drove off."

She paused a moment and wiped her brow.

"I don't think I've ever said this about anyone," she went on, almost wistfully. "But he was almost saintly. And so very nice. But my Lord, he was in a big hurry..."

Chapter Eleven

Sister George told them that when the Jag left the hospital parking lot, it disappeared down the A7—Auxiliary Road 7.

While this route did not lead back to M39 but deeper into the Irish countryside, Sister George was certain the Jag was heading north, towards Ulster.

The Volvo was quickly back in gear and Starr and Maura were soon on the A7 North. It was the narrowest, windiest road they'd traveled yet; the worst curves were marked by yellow blinking lights and looked over by traffic safety cameras. And though the dawn was finally here, it was not yet warm enough to burn off the fog. It was still overcast and cold and the road conditions remained precarious.

Nevertheless, Maura was soon back up to 110 k/h—nearly seventy miles per hour—as they left Galway and followed the A7 into County Mayo, then quickly across to Sligo. The detour at the hospital had slowed them down and burned at least fifteen minutes. But it must have delayed Friendly as well.

One timesaver: there was no longer any need to stop and check the pavement or sniff the air. The math said it all. If the stars stayed aligned, and the priest stayed his course, then the Jag should be just a few miles in front of them. If Maura managed to go just a little bit faster than the smelly sports car, they would catch up to it in less than thirty minutes.

In fact, Maura slowed down only once on this part of the A7. Going around a dangerous bend at a place called Colin's Ridge, she suddenly pulled over to the shoulder and stopped with a screech. An instant later, a Mini Cooper came around the curve, traveling in the opposite direction. It was in the middle of the road, well into their lane. Had Maura not acted when she did, it would have been a high-speed, head-on collision—and the nearby traffic camera would have captured the whole thing.

Once again, Starr couldn't help suspect something like STPA2 was at work. But when he started to say something, Maura gave him a look that needed no translation.

So he told her instead. "I would *so* love to go to the race track with you . . ."

It amazed him how Maura had the ability to carry on a conversation no matter what the situation or the ground speed.

He tried to stay up with her, but sometimes it was hard to do. Luckily, he could never get tired of that accent.

The latest topic for processing was Father Friendly's true motives.

"This guy is supposed to be in league with terrorists," she'd said. "Yet he's doing all these altruistic things—stopping to help the people in the car accident? Blessing the woman at the Grog House? Giving his own victims the Last Rites? There is something so weirdly noble about all that."

Starr couldn't disagree. Father Friendly did not fit a typical profile.

"And it's obvious Sister George has a crush on him . . ." he said dryly.

"So why then," Maura went on, "would someone of his ilk, be giving ten million dollars to a brutal outfit like Ultra IRA?"

"They could be blackmailing him," Starr theorized, rechecking the tightness option on his seat belt. "That's a huge motivation these days."

Maura bit her lip as she took the next curve on two wheels.

"Maybe," she said. "Or maybe it's something else..."

They reached a place called Murphy's Cove just after 8 a.m.

Full daylight was still fifteen minutes away and the fog was still thick. The combination of murk and mist was keeping the visibility down to near zero.

But according to Maura's GPS, they were just twenty miles from the border of Northern Ireland—and the A7 straightened out dramatically at Murphy's Cove. No more twists and turns, no more unexpected dips in the road. Suddenly they were rocketing past fields of over-grown flax and rows of endless peat bogs, with almost no houses and only the occasional wooden bridge.

Starr put his NVGs on as soon as the terrain flattened out. The new model was supposed to be so crazy temper-ature-sensitive, he wondered if he could pick up heat res-idue leftover not from drops of tranny fluid on the ground, but from the Jag's overbearing exhaust system itself.

Again, Starr did the math. Friendly was still at least two miles ahead of them and he had to be matching their speed of 70 MPH or sometimes more. So any heat signa-ture would be faint. But there was so little else out here, even a slight glow in his goggles might indicate some-thing interesting.

About a mile north of Murphy's Cove was a place called Kilkenny Fields. The terrain dropped here by about twenty feet, but the road still went dead straight for the next mile. The change in topography gave Starr the first real opportunity to sweep the landscape with his new NVGs.

At first, he saw just more of the same: a long straight road running through a patchwork of fields and bogs with no crazy heat signatures. But about a mile up ahead, the road began elevating again, leading to not quite a hill, more of a knoll, with trees on either side. From its top, Starr could see four long streams of red light piercing the fog and gloom.

"Wa-da-fa is that?" he exclaimed.

Maura pulled the Volvo to another screeching stop. Starr passed her the NVGs—and then she saw it too. Four streams of red light crackling through the dank morning air.

"OMG," she said excitedly. "That looks like 'War of the Worlds' or something . . ."

Again, Starr couldn't disagree. It did look almost paranormal.

He reached up, activated the NVG's Super Ears app and tapped her twice on the shoulder. Suddenly Maura's hearing was enhanced as well.

That's when she realized the lights were very much of this Earth.

"OMG," she said again. "That's gunfire. Not pop guns either . . ."

She returned his NVGs and started driving again, but not nearly so fast. They both got their weapons ready.

Goggles back on, Starr began a running commentary of what he was seeing.

"Definitely two high caliber weapons at the top of that rise behind the trees," he said, describing the scene now about a half mile away. "Weapons coming in view. Oh, man, two pickup trucks. One on either side of the road. Two fifty-cals in the backs of both."

"Technicals?" Maura asked, surprised. "In Ireland?"

That's what they called them in other parts of the world. Technicals were fast-moving vehicles, usually Toyota pickups, with some big-ass weapon in back. In this case, each truck was carrying a dual-barrel 50-caliber machine gun—so four big guns in all. Just one of these monsters had enough fire power to shoot up a tank or knock down an airplane. One burst would vaporize a human being.

At the moment, the weapons were sweeping the fields in front of them with heavy gunfire, as if they suspected something—or someone—was hiding in the tall flax. As a result, the entire area was lit up with so much heat, it was skewing the NVG electronics.

The guns abruptly stopped firing, though, and their flare went away, restoring full night vision to the NVGs. But just a moment later, the goggles lit up again. There was another burst of heat, this time coming from the side of the road at the bottom of the knoll; a low point still veiled in fog and partially hidden by tall strands of flax, bent over from the heavy morning dew. The splash of light hit Starr's NVGs like an explosion of emerald flame.

When he was able to focus again, he saw it was the exhaust plume from a car engine suddenly coming to life. It was instantly giving off lots of noise and smoke and heat. And even from here they could both smell the hideous odor.

Starr said to Maura: "I think we've just found our Jaguar . . ."

But then the bright red sports car suddenly burst out of the flax and fog; it had been hiding, lying in wait until it was time to make a move.

Now was that time.

The Jag roared up the incline, steering directly for the machine-gun laden trucks, trailing a cloud of hot, smoky exhaust was in its wake. The gun trucks immediately adjusted their aim and began firing at the oncoming car. But the Jag continued its mad dash, undeterred.

It was all happening so quickly, Starr could hardly keep up the continuous report for Maura. "He's driving right at them. Those two doubles are going to dust him. What the hell is he doing? Hold on . . . something new.

I'm getting another flash of light. It looks like more gun-fire—but I think it's coming from the Jag . . ."

It was true. The Jaguar's driver had his right hand out the window and was firing a substantial-sized pistol at the gun trucks on the crest.

In the next two seconds Starr saw the gun trucks trying to re-adjust their aim to fire down at the Jag. But by this time the car was going so fast it went by the technicals like a rocket. Passing over the top of the crest, all four wheels left the ground for a moment and then it was suddenly gone.

In the next second, one of the technicals burst into flame and the other one stopped firing altogether.

It took Starr a few more seconds to figure out what had just happened.

The gun trucks, which they had to assume were in the employ of the Robotov crime family, had set up a near-perfect ambush, expertly pinning-in the road. But their operators hadn't counted on one thing: mechanical night-mare though it was, the 1966 Jaguar E-Type Special-12 was built very low to the ground. Too low for the gunners on the technicals to depress their barrels in enough time to get a clear shot at it.

The Jag made it right between them, apparently un-harmed. But in that same moment, one of the rounds the Jag driver had fired must have somehow miraculously found a target because the dual fifty on the back of one truck inadvertently fired on the other, blowing it to pieces.

By now the surviving technical had backed off the knoll and was driving at high speed across the foggy fields, churning up great mounds of mud behind it.

Maura rolled the Volvo up to the scene a few moments later.

The smoke had nearly enveloped the top of the knoll, and mixed with the fog, it was dense and acrid. The combined stench of cordite and the Jag's exhaust was everywhere.

Starr and Maura didn't even get out of the car. The roadway was littered with pieces of chrome and broken head lights, the glass sparkling like diamonds in the fog. Two large splotches of shiny transmission fluid were also in evidence.

So, the Jag had survived, but it hadn't escaped unscathed.

"This little encounter didn't help his engine issues any," Starr told Maura. "But where are we? Five miles from Ulster? Maybe less?"

She threw back her hair and floored the accelerator.

"Not a problem," she said. "If that's where he's going, then there's still time to catch him."

Chapter Twelve

Five minutes of even wilder driving followed.

The terrain had reverted back to hills and curves and those unexpected Irish dips in the road. But with Maura at the wheel and on the pedal, every turn was traversed via a controlled skid, every hill topped with cool abandon at near 80 MPH. It gave Starr a new appreciation for Swedish-built cars and shock absorbers.

This part was more harrowing than the rest of the trip combined. Still, Starr's only solace was that Maura's driving skills were on full display, not only as a top-notch professional stunt driver, but also an expert in defensive driving. Somewhere deep down in his low-grade terror he trusted her to get them where they had to go in one piece.

Finally, they reached the top of a hill called Marsh's Steep. Beyond it, the A7 went on for another curving mile before ending at a small, half-green, half-orange drawbridge known as Kilcoyne Crossing.

On the other side was Ulster County.

Starr and Maura got incredibly lucky at this point. Because looking down from Marsh's Steep with the NVGs, Starr could see Friendly's Jag pulled to the side of the road a half mile in front of them. Exhaust and other kinds of smoke were pouring from its tailpipe and other places.

Even better, Starr could see Father Friendly, the car hood up, in the process of adding what could only be transmission fluid via a spout near the engine.

It was the first time Starr had ever seen the priest in the flesh so to speak. That he appeared ethereal and ghostly in the electronic, emerald world of NightVision was no surprise. For some reason, Starr was never really convinced this moment would ever happen.

But here they were, he and Maura—and their holy murderous phantom, just a half mile away in a seriously fucked-up car.

By the time Maura started down the hill, Friendly was back inside the Jag and had resumed driving again, but it didn't make any difference. The Jag was dying. It was just barely puttering along the two-lane road, leaving cumulus clouds of exhaust and smoke behind it.

Starr was one breath away from exclaiming "Success!" when his STPA2 kicked in.

Stop!

But Maura had already stood on the brakes, bringing the police car to another screeching, skidding, smoky 360-degree stop.

An instant after that, the road in front of them disappeared in a hail of large caliber weapons fire. Chunks of asphalt and rock went flying in all directions, lots of them hitting the Volvo's hood and roof. More smoke, more flames—horrific, as heard via the Super Ears app, blinding as seen through the NVGs. Had Maura not stopped the car when she did, they would have been vaporized along with the roadway.

The helicopter gunship roared over them a second later, not twenty feet above the roof of the Volvo.

It was a Westland 30, the civilian version of the Lynx military copter. This one was pimped out with 50-mm cannons and rocket launchers, a Russian Hind gunship wannabe. It was spraying the A7 with M-60 cannon fire.

"Wow—they really want that ten million back!" Maura cried above the horrendous noise.

Watching the shells walk right up to the barely moving Jaguar, a flash of helplessness came over Starr and Maura. This is how it ends, they thought together: our mark blown to smithereens right in front of us.

But then . . . no real surprise, something very strange happened.

Father Friendly jumped out of the still-moving Jag, expertly rolled across the narrow roadway, raised a large pistol with both hands and fired off five shots in rapid succession—all in the blink of an eye.

All five rounds hit their intended target: the non-hardened glass of the copter's non-military cockpit, instantly killing the pilots. The aircraft eerily flew along for a few seconds before there was a loud crack of electricity and the engines exploded. The copter banked wildly to the right, went over on its main rotor and plowed into a large peat farm 300 feet off the road.

Another larger, explosion followed. After that, there was nothing but a few flames and a big black hole in the ground.

Starr had never seen anything like it.

Neither had Maura.

"My God," she cried again. "He's Batman!"

The lightning-quick encounter had ended badly for the gunship, its smoking remains already becoming one with the peat bog a football field away.

But the Jag didn't fare much better.

A storm of shrapnel had caught it broadside, perforating it to the extent that it simply rolled to a near-stop— and then toppled over into a ditch.

Starr saw Friendly look down at the smoldering wreck and then take off running across the peat bog, away from the burning copter, heading for the bridge at Kilcoyne Crossing, two white bags in hand.

Maura started driving again, calling her DHQ at the same time. She shouted their position and the situation and asked for instructions.

Meanwhile, by choosing to run along the bogs, Friendly was actually taking the long way to the bridge. The road ran right around the edge of the peat farm and ended in a small roundabout hard by an old border crossing post. If they hurried, Starr and Maura could cut him off before he reached the twin-colored span.

Maura began wheeling her way around the last bit of the A7, which narrowed to a single lane as it led to the bridge. Again, it took some fantastic driving, but soon she screeched to a halt not 20 feet from the crossing.

Just now visible in the slowly lifting fog, Friendly saw he was trapped. Starr jumped out of the car, pointed his weapon at the priest not fifteen feet away and ordered him to stop. But Friendly ignored him and kept on running.

Starr neatly slid across the hood of the Volvo and began to chase the priest on foot, excitedly yelling to Maura to join him.

But she called back to him: *"Wait!"*

Starr skidded to a stop. "Wait?—you mean, let's go!"

As Starr was yelling this, the priest had reached the bridge.

"I can't go," Maura shocked him by saying: "Dublin Central needs to approve me crossing the border."

Starr just looked back at her in disbelief. "You're kidding, right?"

She wasn't.

"It's politics. It might take hours. But I can't go across until then."

"Really?" Starr exclaimed, hurrying back to her. "Come on—we can get him right now . . . who'll know?"

But she didn't move.

"I just can't," she said. "But you can . . ."

That's when Starr realized they had to suddenly part ways.

This was very unexpected.

They almost hugged again—but instead Starr embarrassed himself by awkwardly shaking hands with her.

Then he took off—and began chasing the priest into Ulster by himself.

Chapter Thirteen

The rundown brick building at 32 Terrace Lane in West Belfast was thought to be haunted.

Four stories high and more than two hundred years old, at one time it had housed both a coffin factory *and* a mortuary, giving rise to stories the place was cursed. These days, seemingly fulfilling that reputation, it was a collection of shabby apartments and empty offices.

Madeline McCree had been cleaning the building for forty-four years. Three in the morning to noon, that had been her schedule for four decades and she kept to it religiously.

In addition to being spooky, Terrace Lane was in a bad part of Belfast, not that there were many good parts. On first encountering Maddie, people would frequently ask that, with her advanced age, wasn't this a chancy place to be employed? But then they'd meet Bear, Maddie's all-white Pyrenees-Wolfhound-Malamute mix, and they'd understand.

Bear was gigantic and warm and cuddly—until he sensed any kind of threat to Maddie. Then he earned his nickname. He'd been with Maddie at all times, on the job and off, for the past ten years. After a few pints, she was known to call him her guardian angel.

It was now 8:30 a.m.; outside, the weather was still cold and rainy. Maddie and Bear reached the third floor of the building where she retrieved a fresh mop from a closet at the top of the stairs. There were ten office suites up here, all of them empty. That made no difference to her. She cleaned each one, five days a week, no matter what.

She'd just filled her mop bucket when Bear started to growl. Down the hall, a light was on in one of the empty offices.

This shouldn't be. No one was supposed to be in any of them.

Bear inched slowly towards the office, nose to the floor, snarling with every step, Maddie behind him. She pushed the door open with the end of her mop . . . and saw something from a nightmare.

Standing in the middle of the empty office, three heavily armed men were strangling a fourth man with an electrical cord. The victim was tied to a chair, had been brutally beaten and was soaked in blood and bile. Maddie detected a priest's collar entwined in the electrical cord.

Behind them, a man was lying dead beneath a broken window. Another figure, also dead, was hanging halfway out the same window, his body badly cut by broken glass.

Maddie saw all this in just a few seconds—two things happened next. One of the men yanked on the mop, pulling Maddie into the room and slamming the door behind her—locking Bear out. Then a second man hit her so hard across the face, she was flung backwards, crashing against the wall.

Bear began barking furiously outside the door, his paws scratching wildly on the frame. Stepping over Maddie's convulsing body, the third man screwed a silencer onto his pistol and fired four shots through the door.

Bear stopped barking.

The gunmen were Russians in the pay of the Robotov crime family. Their assignment was simple. Kill Father Friendly and retrieve their employer's $10 million.

But it had been a messy operation from the start. The Albanians previously hired by the Robotovs had screwed the pooch bigtime on four separate occasions: at the A7 ambush spot, at the Grog House, in Shawnsbridge and with the helicopter attack, once again proving you get what you pay for.

But now these pure Russian gunmen—supposedly experts, they'd arrived from Moscow just two hours before—were the ones on the verge of completely botching the operation.

Working on intelligence hacked from SDU's Dublin Central HQ, five of them had accosted the priest just minutes after he arrived in Ulster, spiriting him to this virtually empty building in West Belfast with plans to strangle him. But on arrival, the priest put up such a monumental fight, he killed two of their colleagues via lightning-quick kicks to the throat. Many more punches were thrown before the remaining three gunmen were able to subdue him.

Maddie presented a further complication. Their plan called for getting rid of just one body: Father Friendly. Now, once the priest and the cleaning lady had been dispatched, they'd be stuck with four stiffs, not counting the dead dog outside the door.

The Robotovs didn't like complications. In their dark netherworld, any bungled assignment usually required a job reevaluation and they were never pleasant. (In many ways, the cut-rate Albanians were lucky they were dead.) The stress of knowing this black reality had become so overwhelming, one of the Russian gunmen confessed he was on the verge of a *panicheskaya ataka*. Having a panic attack.

The jittery assassins had a quick discussion. Time was their greatest enemy at the moment. They were convinced that strangling the priest would now take too long. Even though he was tied, and bloody and gasping for air, anytime they tried to tighten the electrical cord around his neck, he would put up a tremendous struggle, fighting them off and making a lot of commotion.

So even though their employer had specifically ordered the holy man be choked—slowly—the gunmen were going to default on that part of the contract.

Their decision: One silencer bullet for him, one for the old lady. Then they were going to take the money, blow up the place and hope that the Robotovs didn't delve too deeply into how the priest met his end.

But a knock on the door changed everything.

Before the Russian assassins could move, the door swung open and two men calmly walked into the room. Black eyes, hardened faces, Scally caps. Both carrying massive .44 Magnums at their sides.

They were members of the Ultra-IRA.

"Marky Conley sent us," one man said, looking around the room then closing the door behind him. "So, let's all stay cool."

The Russians took the advice and remained frozen. Though tough guys themselves, they'd heard about the ultra-violent UIRA and wanted no part of this pair. Plus, they were sure other Supermicks were waiting nearby.

The two terrorists walked around the room in a deliberate and menacing manner. One had a hideous scar that went from ear to ear.

"You've helped us out here, I see," he said, examining the barely breathing priest. "Done half our job for us. That's good. So, here's your reward. We don't want the money. You guys take it back to your employer. We just need the priest to come with us. Our bosses would like to chat with him before he hits the Great Beyond. Any objections?"

The three Russians shook their heads as one. They were all for it.

The second UIRA member took out an old flip phone and called someone. He said: "Bring the truck around and bring up the bag."

Meanwhile the man with the scar spotted the two dead bodies and asked: "And what happened here?"

One of the Russians nodded towards the battered, semi-conscious priest. "He kicks in throat," he explained in broken English. "They get in way of his foot."

The Irish terrorist looked down at Maddie, crumpled on the floor.

"And the coot?"

The Russian nudged her body with his foot. "As you say, 'collateral damage . . .'"

The second UIRA man made another call.

"Make that four bags," he said.

A moment later, there was a syncopated knock on the door. The UIRA man with the phone opened it and started to say: "Do you know we need four bags for . . ." but the words never really made it out of his mouth.

Bear the dog came right at him, teeth to his throat, tearing through flesh and bone. Starr was right behind him, throwing a running block against three of the men in the room. Rolling on the floor, he grabbed Maddie by the shoulders and slid her out the open door. Bear quickly followed and Starr slammed the door shut behind them.

Then the bullets started flying—but in the cramped, suddenly explosive office, having STPA2 paid off for him. Starr had his pistol out, but he hadn't needed to shoot it yet. Instead he was listening to his inner voice and going where it was telling him to go, which was out of the path of any on-coming bullets.

Others in the room weren't so lucky. Two of the Russians took bullets to their skulls in the crossfire, and the surviving UIRA man sustained wounds to his hand.

But in the midst of the melee, the priest's chair was thrown backwards—and came down hard on top of Starr's head, knocking them both out cold.

Chapter Fourteen

Starr woke up tied back to back with Father Friendly on two chairs pushed together.

At his feet were the bodies of two Russian hired guns and the UIRA member whose throat had been torn out by Maddie's guardian angel.

Head still buzzing, Starr saw one Irish gunman and one Russian assassin were left standing. Father Friendly was still alive, but just barely. Starr could feel his labored breathing against his back; blood from his various wounds was dripping on the floor. Outside, the sun was fully up, those few rays piercing the overcast glittering off the jagged glass of the broken window-pane.

The UIRA member was on speaker on his cell. Obviously, some plans had changed. He was talking about videos and bombs and who should get the footage once Father Friendly and Starr were dead.

An email address was mentioned. Then the UIRA man walked over to Starr and the priest and began taking copious video of them. That's the first time Starr noticed the homemade bomb on the floor next to his right foot.

It was a big one. At least a half-pound of plastique attached to a coffee can filled with jellied gasoline. It was enough firepower to take out the whole block.

Videos sent, the UIRA man set the timer on the bomb. Then he received one last order from his superiors, once again, heard loud and clear over the phone's speaker.

"Give them both a bow tie first," the eerily detached brogue said. "And take video of it. The boss wants to make sure . . ."

Starr knew what that meant; it was underworld lingo for slicing a throat. A second later he heard the unmistakable sound of a knife being unsheathed.

But . . . just then he became aware of something else.

Looking through the broken window he could see, on the next roof over, Maura, Maddie and Bear, looking back at him. Next to them were three Ulster cops. One was pointing a rifle at Starr's head. It had a telescopic sight attached.

Maura was looking right at him; her eyes telling him all he needed to know. One or both of their assailants were going to cut his throat in the next few seconds. The police sniper would not have a clear shot with Starr and Father Friendly in the way.

If Starr could just move at the right moment . . .

Maura's eyes were asking him for the go-ahead.

He braced himself, then mouthed two words: "Do it . . ."

The two bullets came through the hole in the window and struck the UIRA man and the Russian assassin in their skulls almost simultaneously. Two perfect kill shots—but only because an instant before the sniper squeezed his trigger, Starr used all his strength to push him and Father Friendly over—and out of the way of the sniper's bullets.

They landed in another heap, crashing back onto the floor, their would-be executioners falling like deadweights right next to them.

Then, everything went quiet.

They were still alive—and somehow Maura had saved them.

But he still had the bomb at his feet.

Starr wiggled out of his plastic ties and studied the device. This was not a nail-bomb. It was pure high explosive, with so much gooey plastique and gasoline jelly, it was oozing out of the sides.

Starr had been trained in explosive ordinance disposal. He knew the best approach was the Zen-approach.

Be methodical.

Be centered.

Be the bomb.

But he also knew, at that moment, crouched next to the overflowing canister, that he didn't have much time before this baby went off.

Ten seconds . . . his inner voice confirmed.

Possibly enough time to escape the building before it went up—but he wasn't going to leave Father Friendly behind.

He managed to open the top of the bomb, uncovering a spaghetti tangle of wires.

Seven seconds, turned to six and then five.

He didn't have a knife, he couldn't cut anything; besides, it was such a jumble, he had no idea which wires needed to be disconnected . . .

Four seconds . . . three . . .

Pull them all . . .

He froze for an instant knowing that sometimes he could almost fool himself into thinking he could hear his inner voice when it was convenient.

Was this one of those times?

Two . . . one . . .

He reached in and gave all of the wires a yank. A second after that, one of them started sparking wildly before fizzling out.

That one was the fuse.

The rest? Who knew?

And who cared?

He freed Father Friendly, laying the brutally beaten priest on the floor and covering him with his jacket. But the priest threw it off him and tried to get up.

"I must perform Extreme Unction on these men," he gasped, just barely able to talk. "I must give all of them the Last Rites."

Starr gently nudged the priest back down to the floor.

"I have to tell you, father, that's really noble," he said. "But with this crew, I don't think it's going to do any good."

Chapter Fifteen

Sister George was surprised when Starr and Maura walked back into her emergency room later that morning. She'd been on her feet nearly twenty-four hours, every minute of it busy, and never gave the couple another thought.

But the nun was truly shocked when she saw the man they were carrying between them was the same generous, saintly man she'd met earlier in the night.

He'd been so handsome back then, and well-dressed from what she could see. Now, wrapped in a dirty car blanket, he was obviously badly injured and needed assistance just to stay on his feet.

The walk-in ward was still overcrowded with accident victims. But sensing the special circumstances, Sister George directed the three through a set of doors and into an empty hospital room.

Starr and Maura carefully lowered the priest onto the bed. Only then was Sister George able to examine him. She pulled away the car blanket and gasped. She'd seen her share of injuries over thirty years, but Friendly's were among the worst. He was bloody, he had multiple fractures, dozens of ligature marks around his neck, and the pallor of someone close to death.

The nun had just assumed his race car had been in an accident. But it was clear the man had been beaten and so horribly choked, the blood vessels had burst in his eyes.

"What happened to him?" the nun asked them.

Maura shook her head and told her. "I'm sorry, that's classified . . ."

But the nun's wrinkled face turned dark. Many of the man's wounds had already begun to bruise over. The injuries had been inflicted more than an hour ago.

"Then what's he doing here?" she demanded to know. "Why hasn't he got medical attention before now?"

Maura looked to Starr, who just shrugged.

The young detective took the nun's hand and told her softly: "Sister, he wanted to die in Galway. It's part of a plea agreement. And we'd appreciate your cooperation."

A deal had been worked out via a scrambled phone call between the Chief of the Ulster Police, the director of SDU's Dublin Central and Starr's boss at ONI, the Admiral himself.

The Ulster cops would clean up the mess left at Terrace Lane. They would also take possession of the $10 million and eventually divide it up to local charities throughout Northern Ireland who served the sort of people, who, as it turns out, Father Friendly wanted to help.

In return, SDU Dublin Central agreed to form a joint strike force with the Ulster police to identify the UIRA members who'd been involved in the episode and then break up the terrorist cell before it grew any bigger.

Both sides also agreed to forget the fact that Maura had entered Northern Ireland against protocol. As it turned out, all were glad she did. Finally getting frustrated with no word back from Dublin SDU, she drove across the bridge at Kilcoyne Crossing, and followed her "guardian angel" to Terrace Lane where she ran into Maddie and Bear. A quick call to the Ulster cops brought out their SWAT unit—and the rest was history.

Starr had arrived at the Belfast location by more conventional means. He'd witnessed the priest being abducted by the Russian gunmen on the other side of the bridge. With only a moment of hesitation, he'd bravely hailed a cab and literally told the driver to "follow that car."

As it turned out, the timing of the climax couldn't have been more down to the wire. And some really bad actors were no longer among the living.

But then there was one last issue that needed to be resolved: Father Friendly turned out to be hero of sorts, or delusional. While waiting for the Ulster cops to reach them after he'd defused the bomb, the priest had told Starr this story: He'd woken up in the middle of the night a week ago, suffering from a ferocious headache and experiencing vivid flashbacks of his time in Iraq and Afghanistan. Reliving the instances of death and horror he'd seen became so intense he lost his sight.

Convinced he was dying, he lay back down and simply waited for the end. But Friendly had a vision instead. A strange one, but simple enough. He said an angel appeared to him and told him if he went to the nearby Encore Casino four nights hence, he would win big, be approached by someone running a high stakes poker game—and win big again.

But he had to vow to spend the money he won in the right way.

Friendly said he got on his knees and made that vow. The headache and the flashbacks immediately stopped, and he got his sight back.

And that's why he was in Ireland.

British Intelligence *had* gotten it wrong from the start. He wasn't funding terrorists. He was passing the money on to their victims—both Catholic and Protestant—families who'd lost loved ones, and in a lot of cases, lost hope too during the inter-religious squabbles of years past.

"Many of the children who grew up at the tail end of that are now young adults and really troubled souls," the priest had told them between gasps of air as they sped back into the Republic, Starr driving, Maura with Friendly in the back seat, trying to keep him from going into shock.

"They need to realize that even though their childhood was a nightmare, the rest of their life doesn't need to be," Friendly had continued. "I saw it in Afghanistan and I saw it in Iraq. If something good doesn't happen in these peoples' lives by the age of thirty, then most of them are lost causes. It's my duty to help prevent that. It's my duty to give them hope."

"As a priest?" Starr had asked him at the time.

"As a human being," Friendly had replied.

For the Admiral's part, after hearing the details of the case, he was able to get all sides on the phone call to agree that Starr could take custody of the injured priest and "transport the prisoner at his discretion."

Friendly had told them both his parents could trace their roots back to multiple generations of living in the Galway section of the Irish Republic. That's why he'd taken the bizarre route earlier. He wanted to drive through the place his family had called home for generations—thinking then that it was most likely for the last time.

But it would not be. Not quite.

That's why they were back at Galway Memorial Hospital.

Sister George injected Friendly with morphine, started a saline IV drip and, with Starr's help, was able to put an oxygen mask on him. But none of it did any good. The priest was going in and out of consciousness, his face turning a disturbing blue whenever he was out.

Sister George injected him with Lidocaine, directly into his heart, literally bringing him back to life. But it was clear the priest didn't have much time left.

In this fading lucid moment, Friendly pushed the oxygen mask aside and asked Starr and Maura to come closer. There were things that they should know.

First off, and most surprising, he revealed he'd intentionally rented the bad Jag because he knew only other special operators would know how to track one.

"You were my back-up," he told them weakly. "I knew I was going to run into some rough characters if I landed in the south and drove north, but that's just the way I had to do it because I didn't want to get clipped walking off the plane at Belfast Airport.

"But I also knew the intelligence agencies would send people after me. And I'll always be grateful it turned out to be you two."

He closed his eyes and coughed heavily.

"And thank you for bringing me back here," he said, his voice just a whisper. "It's a little thing I suppose. I've never even been in Ireland before. But I feel warm inside now that I am here. Or maybe it's the morphine."

He pointed to his valise, carried in with them from the car. Starr fished around inside—and came out with a small bottle of oil and a packet of salt.

The instruments of the Last Rites.

"Please," he asked them. "After what's happened, I'm going to need all the help I can get."

Sister George performed the ritual, and for the first time, Friendly really seemed to relax; the inherent intensity was suddenly gone. His whole body went limp, but he was smiling.

He thanked them again and then closed his eyes, waiting for his time to finally be up.

Maura was holding his hand; Starr and Sister George pulled up chairs next to the bed.

"We will not let him die alone," the nun whispered to them, blessing herself. "I believe he deserves more than that."

A serene peace descended on the room. Such a strange case, Starr thought. Such an unusual hero . . .

But suddenly, the peace was broken. Suddenly Friendly was trying to sit up and tell them something else, but failing at both. The burst of energy startled them; possibly the last effects of the Lidocaine. He fell back onto the bed, but continued to struggle to say something.

Finally he was able to gasp: "You should know how I was able to win the ten million so easily in the first place. *Someone* should know how I did it . . ."

Maura put her ear to his lips. Starr came in close too.

But before the priest could say another word, he took one last breath—and died.

Chapter Sixteen

Starr and Maura talked non-stop the entire two-hour drive back to Dublin.

No M39, M20 or A7—this time, it was a straight shot south, all the way on the A1.

The Case of Father Friendly dominated the first part of the journey. The money. The Jag. The Albanians. Technicals, gunships, nail bombs, big dogs, Russians, and cleaning ladies—and finally a highly trained sniper.

But none of it mystified them more than the priest's last words. How does one win ten million dollars easily?

About halfway to the capital, the conversation changed as the case faded from view. Starr learned that Maura came from a long line of policemen and she'd given up a full scholarship to Trinity College to become a cop herself—and help her brother's small startup electronics company.

She mentioned, almost as an aside, that she'd managed to get him some work with the SDU. But before Starr could ask for further details, she steered the conversation back in his direction by asking him a loaded question: What's the best thing about America?

The ride south went by much faster compared to their long journey north the night before. In many ways, Starr didn't want it to end.

But at last they pulled up in front of a totally unremarkable Quonset-type building in a small undistinctive business park in the Dublin neighborhood of Swords. It was not far from the Dublin airport.

"This is headquarters," Maura told him. "My DHQ . . ."

A closer look revealed the building was heavily weather-beaten and squeaked mightily in the wind. But its roof was festooned with dozens of radio antennas, satellite dishes and other electronic clutter. Long strands of electrical cords and coaxial wires ran into the hut's side windows.

Interestingly, the building was painted a light shade of green.

They went inside to a small lobby. A desk, three chairs and an old rotary phone. That was it. It was threadbare, sterile and surprisingly dull.

Maura turned to face him, taking off her coat, and taking his to hang up.

And it was at that moment that Starr finally realized just who Maura's guardian angel was.

He reached over—and pulled a quarter from behind her right ear. He handed the coin to her; she looked up at him quizzically.

"Strange time for a magic trick," she said.

He then revealed what was in his other hand.

It was her Angel earring. But at the moment, the two tiny emerald pin lights were not pulsating. Instead they were glowing steady. That was the only clue he needed.

On seeing the earring, Maura's hands immediately went to her crucifix, which was actually a miniscule microphone, just as the earring was a cleverly disguised, miniature radio receiver. Blinking lights usually meant the signal was there, but intermittent. Steady lights indicated the radio receiver was very, very close by.

"Did you buy all this on eBay?" he asked her dryly.

Twin looks of shock and embarrassment came across her pretty features.

But then she laughed.

"We thought an Irish girl praying to her crucifix would be a good cover," she told him.

"It was," he replied truthfully. "You had me believing it . . ."

She came up close to him and playfully tugged on his jacket.

"Say it," she ordered him, still laughing. "Say the words. Say I fooled you."

He laughed too. He couldn't help it. She was gorgeous and funny, a rare combination.

"Please don't make me," he pleaded.

She let him go—but only after she took back her earring.

She examined it closely. The earring back was reattached to the pin, which immediately got her thinking, how did he take it from her ear in the first place?

He knew what she was going to ask him, so he gave her a pre-emptive shrug.

"I swear those are the only two tricks I know . . ." he said.

"You better not be lying to me," she replied, giving him another swipe on the arm. "Unless you think seeing in the dark is a trick."

He started to say something, but stopped. What did she mean by that?

Thankfully, she changed the subject.

"You know our secret now anyway," she told him. "So, do you want to see the brains?"

"I can't wait," he replied.

She led him into the next room—and it was like walking into another world.

It was one, large open space cluttered with a fantastic amount of electronics. Hundreds of radio receivers, amplifiers, TV monitors, speakers, piles of them stacked on top of each other and tethered in by Gordian knots of cables, coaxial wires and power cords. It was all lit by dozens of recessed blue, red and green LED lights hidden away in the most unusual and unlikely places.

Looking like something from a really low-budget James Bond film, it had its own beauty to it, chaos art.

She led him over the mounds of cables and brought him to console panel at the far end of the room. Here, sat a man of about thirty who Starr imagined to be a real Irish geek. His pocket protector was festooned with a tie-dye shamrock. The console itself was covered with dozens of smaller electronic gadgets, microphones, mini-TV cameras and more speakers. It was such a mess it too was almost artistic; not 007, more like a Star Trek episode on mushrooms.

"This is my brother, Finny," Maura said. "If anyone asks, he's officially working as an electronics intern for the SDU. Unofficially he's my guardian angel."

Starr stuck out his hand and introduced himself, saying he worked for the U.S. Navy.

Finny stood up and nervously shook Starr's hand. But then he looked at Maura as if to say, what's going on here?

"He knows," she told him simply. "He figured it out."

There was a muffled conversation between the siblings; not many people even knew this place existed.

But Starr wasn't paying attention. He became mesmerized by the very large TV screen, 96-inches at least, hanging on the far wall of the building, about ten feet from the console.

On it was what could only be described as a living, pulsing, moving map of Ireland. It took him almost a full minute to figure out exactly what it was. It literally looked like it was alive, a moving, shimmering thing.

Then it started to make sense to him. This place that Maura called her DHQ was about tapping into what Starr could only imagine were thousands of video cameras scattered throughout Ireland. In the cities, in the country, along every highway—all of these video feeds had been electronically overlapped to create the living map. Overhead shots prevailed, but if something seemed to be happening below, it would automatically shift to that view.

"Algorithms," Starr sighed. "They're behind everything."

"She's the one who called it the Guardian Angel," Finny explained in a very thick brogue. "It works by combining everything from local security cameras to GO-Pros to spy satellites. It also doubles as a tracking device that has contact on her crucifix 24/7. Her handler can tell her, via the earring speaker, what to do, how to avoid an immediate situation and so on. So, when it's working perfectly, it can give the appearance that she's two steps ahead of the game. It's perfect for undercover work."

Starr was greatly impressed. "And you're her handler?"

Finny relaxed, smiled and took a bow. "That would be me," he confirmed.

This wasn't just some geek's dream, Starr was realizing. This was a highly advanced individual doing his final college project before going on to dazzle someone in the spy world.

Of course, it was all highly illegal. It had to be against some kind of privacy law, but that never stopped intelligence services before, even two-person ones.

Though taking the longest route possible, this conglomeration ended up to be in a pretty impressive place: it was better than ninety-percent of the video feeds Starr had seen from military spy satellites.

Finny pulled his smart phone from his pocket protector and showed it to Starr. It was displaying the same pulsing, living map, reduced to a mobile screen.

Starr was blown away. "This little app can do all that?"

Standing patiently nearby, Maura punched him again. And this one hurt.

"This little app?" she said in that voice. "I'll tell you it's a very valuable piece of electronic equipment, developed after years of research. And they cost a fortune."

Starr took the angel earring from her again and examined it more closely. It *was* exquisite. Then, he looked around at the mad scientist laboratory and nodded in agreement.

She was right. The sum of the parts was beautiful in a Bizarro-world kind of way. And it had nothing to do with ESP.

"I can understand that now," he said. "Angels aren't cheap . . ."

They sat in the lobby and ate stew Finny had cooked and coffee Maura had ground herself. They talked for hours, nonstop. There was never a break in the conversation and there were lots of laughs. Especially from Maura who was *really* funny.

But the Cosmos had one last punchline to deliver to Starr.

Maura had excused herself to get more coffee; Finny just happened to mention that Starr was lucky to have survived driving all over Ireland the night before.

"The weather comes as advertised," he replied. "But I don't think I've seen fog so thick." Finny laughed. "I'm not talking about the fog. I'm talking about her behind the wheel. She's the absolutely worst driver in the world. Has no idea what the brake pedal is."

Starr felt his face drain of color as the delayed reaction horror set in.

Suddenly, Maura reappeared with more coffee and some cake, smiling, but instantly picking up on his distress.

"What did he tell you about me?" she growled, pointing at Finny.

"That you used to sneak nips of whiskey when we were kids," the brother replied coolly.

Maura immediately relaxed.

"Is that all?" she said smiling.

Starr wanted it to go on forever—but as it always seems to happen in these things, his cell phone started beeping at the worst possible moment. It was the Admiral's office, telling him they'd blessed his preliminary report, considered the case closed and were calling him home. A cab was on the way, just like his flight, courtesy of the CIA. He had to be at Dublin Airport in twenty minutes.

It took Maura by surprise too. He could tell she'd wished it would never end either.

She hastily packed up some cake to take with him. Then Finny shook his hand and excused himself, disappearing back into the DHQ, leaving them alone in the small, spare lobby.

"This is the second time we've said goodbye," he told her, putting his jacket and cap back on, and grabbing his gig bag.

"Well, at least this one won't be so hurried," she said.

Then came that awful moment that falls between a handshake or a hug. Always awkward, never coordinated—and Starr was really bad at them.

But this one was different.

Because Maura simply fell into his arms and they embraced . . . for a long time.

The cab ride to Dublin Airport was uneventful; it didn't matter. Starr was suddenly exhausted and too deep into his thoughts to even notice any further maniacal driving.

He met the CIA Gulfstream at the airport's U.S. diplomatic gate and was soon on his way back across the puddle at near the speed of sound.

He fell asleep a few times, but only in fits. It always took a while to get back to reality after going through an especially intense case. This one was right up there.

About halfway across the Atlantic, he heard a beeping coming from his gig bag. His cell phone was pulsing.

For one split-second he wondered if for some crazy reason, it might be Maura . . .

But it wasn't.

It was Angel.

She was getting ready for bed and hoped she'd be able to talk to him before she went to sleep. He'd given her an old sat phone—so bulky they called it the Tomato Can—which allowed her to tap into the Navy's classified sat-com link and talk to him anywhere in the world. He'd told her many times to use it only in a dire emergency, but she treated it more or less like her personal phone, something the Navy would be very upset about.

But in this case, he was very happy she called. Just hearing her voice would help bring him back to the real world.

He frequently talked to her about his cases—another gross security violation—but other times he didn't, and when he didn't, she never pried.

That was the case this time.

He gave her the briefest, thumbnail version possible and basically said, all's well that ends well.

In the meantime, she sent him a selfie—worth another couple years at Leavenworth. She was lying on her bed, skimpy nightgown, her fingers running down her cheeks, simulating tears.

She'd labeled it: "I miss Chris."

He took a good long look at the photo and then deleted it. It was useless to remind her about the security violations they were committing. It was best just to get rid of the evidence.

It was a ten-minute conversation, and he could tell she was drifting off to sleep. And now maybe he could too, back on Earth after talking to her.

But he had to ask her one more question.

"Does someone named Angel have a guardian angel?"

She didn't hesitate an instant.

"I have a guardian angel," she told him, sleepily.

"You do?"

"Of course, I do," she said. "My guardian angel is you . . ."

Book Two

The Sea of Moons

Chapter One

San Diego

Starr's cell phone rang at exactly 8 a.m., Pacific Time.

He didn't need his ESP to know the call was coming. He'd been expecting it.

Angel was sitting at her make-up table across the bedroom, wearing a short bathrobe and nothing else. She was smiling at him with anticipation, fingers crossed even while drying her nails.

Starr answered the phone. It was his big boss, the head of ONI's Investigation Division, Admiral Hawley himself.

He was getting a new case. The Admiral gave him a few details including location and timing; further information would be sent via secure email. As usual, Starr was reminded that, like all his other cases, this assignment was classified. He should discuss it with no one.

The moment the Admiral hung up, Starr wrote a single word on a piece of paper, got up and handed it to Angel.

She uncrossed her fingers, opened it and read it aloud: "Tahiti."

A shiver of excitement went through her. But she quickly calmed down, took a deep breath and then dialed her own phone.

Her conversation took twice as long and was much friendlier—but in the end, the result was the same. She hung up, jumped into his arms and kissed him hard on the mouth.

"That was almost too easy," she said.

Two hours later, they were sitting in first class on a Cathay Pacific jumbo jet, heading for paradise.

Starr had heard rumors an assignment in Tahiti was coming his way. Meanwhile, Angel's modeling agency had been begging her for months to do a photo shoot somewhere in the South Pacific.

Though Starr had broken security laws by revealing where he was going to her, all it took was one phone call from Angel and *LA Cosmo* immediately set up a cover-photo shoot at Ora Beach, Tahiti's most luxurious resort.

They both lived hectic lives. Many times they found themselves in different parts of the globe, thousands of miles away from each other.

So this would be their version of a working vacation.

Starr's new case was straightforward.

A long-distance Offshore Powerboat Race was set to go off from Papeete, Tahiti, the following day. The object was to get to Moru One, an island about 350 miles to the west and then return. Shortest time wins.

The contest was an annual event, bringing lots of high-end powerboat manufacturers and fans to the islands. Equipped with monstrous twin engines, the double-hulled racers could reach speeds of 220 MPH or sometimes more. Under the right conditions, the 700-mile trip could take less than five hours. First place prize was $5 million.

ONI's problem: Mercury, the manufacturer of the XB-44, hands-down the best powerboat engine in the world, was about to sign a top-secret deal with the U.S. Navy to supply engines for a new fleet of gunboats for the SEALs. But two weeks before, Mercury contacted ONI with information that Chinese spies were planning to steal an XB-44 engine sometime during the race with the intention of pulling it apart and taking all its secrets.

Starr's job was to go undercover as the driver of the only powerboat equipped with XB-44s. With eyes and ears open, he would be on the lookout for any Chinese mischief and make sure they didn't steal the top dog engine.

Though it was another breech of the Security Act, this is how he explained it all to Angel on the flight over.

"Your job is to look beautiful for one afternoon," he told her. "My job is to go for a motorboat ride. When you're done, just lie in the sun until I can join you."

Chapter Two

Starr's boat was called the *Temiti-Novula*, Tahitian for "The Sea of Moons."

It was a 52-foot long, banana-yellow catamaran with orange flame decals accenting its twin bows. The two ginormous XB-44 engines were hanging off its back; each could produce 1100-horsepower. No surprise the boat could easily hit 200 knots, or about one mile every seventeen seconds.

Its control panel was right out of a modern airliner. No buttons, switches or levers; everything was run by touchscreens, including the AI-based propulsion systems. Steering and throttles were both on the same joystick and were also AI-assisted.

Still, driving the thing meant dealing with substantial g-forces and spine-crushing bouncing, all while getting drenched with tons of sea spray. The boat's open cockpit was about two-thirds down its hull, and, even though there was a good-sized windshield surrounding it, wearing goggles, a crash helmet and a safety suit similar to those worn by F-1 racecar drivers—and also done in bright banana-yellow—was required to help protect him from the 220 MPH counter-wind coming his way.

Powerboat racing was a lot like off-road racing. The track was ever changing, so you had to be thinking ahead at all times. Hitting a wave just right—or wrong—could send the boat flying twenty feet or more in the air. The higher you went, the harder it was when you came back down. Traveling on a high-speed pogo stick with the spray from a powerful showerhead hitting you in the face—that was powerboat racing.

Starr had driven powerboats during a TDY with the SEALs. But the SEAL boats were nothing like this.

Still, just twenty minutes into the race, the *Temiti-Novula* was way out ahead of the pack.

After another twenty minutes, Starr had lost sight of four of the eight other racers. Ten minutes after that, the other four entries faded into the morning haze.

Suddenly he was out in front, all alone.

Around the end of the second hour, he began wondering if he might be succeeding a little too much. Did the Admiral want the *Temiti-Novula* to actually win the race? Nothing in Starr's orders said he shouldn't come in first, but truth was, the race's outcome was never discussed. Keeping the XB-44 out of unfriendly hands was the main objective.

At least Starr was doing that. The Chinese couldn't steal anything as long as the XB-44s were attached to the boat and he was doing those 200 knots. But he'd traveled *so* fast, he was now in the middle of nowhere, out of sight of anywhere and anybody, with nothing but the coral blue sea around him.

If someone really wanted to get nasty, he'd sailed into the perfect spot for an ambush.

The competition's rules stated that on-board radios could be used only in an emergency and that communication between racers was strictly forbidden. Once they'd dropped out of sight, Starr could still keep track of his opponents by calling up a satellite view on his touchscreen. Now, he checked this sat-screen regularly, confirming what he already knew: He was way, *way* out in front, winning the race by a wide margin.

And still, all alone.

About an hour away from Moru One, he habitually looked at the sat-view again. But this time, he saw nothing but a blank screen.

Even from space, none of the other racers were in sight.

A bad feeling washed over him. The voice inside him agreed.

This is too easy . . .

He looked down at his communications suite and realized the entire unit had gone dark. Punching its touchscreen a few dozen times did nothing. It was dead.

Just like that, he had no radio.

If he was going to be ambushed and his assailants were able to somehow glitch his communications, then this was when it would happen. Another boat. A helicopter. A lone fighter plane. He took a moment between wave bounces to reach into his gig bag and pull out his SIG Sauer P266 travel pistol, even as he was saying to himself: "Nothing out here to shoot but the fish . . ."

That's when he heard the ring of an old-fashioned office desk phone.

He reached back into his bag and this time came out with the Tomato Can, his near-obsolete U.S. Navy—issued satellite phone. As far as he knew, there was only one other of its kind still in use around the world. That meant there was only one person who could be calling him on it.

"Hi, Angel . . ." he answered, ducking another mountain of sea spray. "You know you're not supposed to use this phone."

"Chris? Are you there?" she was saying, catching him in mid-sentence.

Starr heard something in her voice. It was not the usual pleasant song. Far from it.

"Honey, what's wrong?" he asked urgently.

"We just had a bad earthquake here," she told him. "I'm OK and everyone on the shoot is OK. But everything shook for almost a minute—one of the longest minutes of my life. Now there are fires everywhere, there are cracks in the street and the power is out."

"Jesuzz, Angel, *are* you OK? Just tell me . . ."

"I am," she reassured him. "It's you I'm worried about. They have a shortwave radio here and it's saying the quake might have been caused by an undersea volcano that's about to erupt . . ." she stopped for a long moment, and then added: "And I think you might be very close to it."

"But it's nothing but clear sailing out here," he told her, still bouncing along at 200 knots. "I'm fine . . ."

Angel wasn't buying it though.

"Chris—please listen carefully," she said in such a way, Starr could almost hear her holding back the tears. "What's your current position?"

Luckily his Can's GPS was still working, though the screen was jumping with static.

"Heading due west," he replied. "Towards Moru One . . ."

Now, in a very determined voice, she told him: "Chris . . . look behind you, out on the horizon. What do you see?"

Starr did as she asked—and that's when he felt like he'd been hit by a hammer.

"Damn . . ." he half whispered.

From one end of the horizon to the other was a wall of dark gray water thirty feet high, roiling beneath a storm of sea spray.

A tsunami . . .

Coming right at him.

Chapter Three

Papeete Harbor
Tahiti

The tidal wave hit Papeete thirty minutes later.

It came as one, giant surge, smashing into the harbor's northwest seawall and flooding large parts of the downtown business district.

But it was only a glancing blow. The wave had come out of the west, meaning the western reaches of the dumbbell-shaped island had borne the brunt of the tsunami. So, even though a large section of Papeete was still ankle deep in water, the roads were jammed with emergency vehicles, klaxons blaring, heading towards the more heavily damaged areas of the island.

Angel had seen the tsunami coming.

Still wearing the bikini she'd been modeling prior to the earthquake, she'd called Starr on the Tomato Can to warn him of the tidal wave, but then lost contact with him. One moment they were talking, the next he wasn't there anymore. She'd tried desperately to get him back, but with no success. It was as if someone pulled the plug on them.

So, throwing on a beach wrap, she'd hurried out of the Ora Beach resort and started making her way through the rubble, determined to get to Papeete, two miles away. She'd prayed the whole time that the race officials would be able to contact his powerboat.

She was on a high beach road about a half mile out from the capital when the wave appeared. One minute it was way out on the horizon, looking like something from a nightmare. The next it was sweeping through the harbor, upsetting dozens of yachts and cruise liners before finally impacting on the beachfront's seawall. This caused a sort-of counterwave, almost as tall and violent, that then rolled back out to sea.

Angel had stood transfixed watching it all, and wondering too if she was somehow caught up in a bad dream.

It took her another thirty minutes to get to the harbor and reach the headquarters of the Offshore Power Boat Racing Association.

Its lobby was flooded with water, but a sympathetic employee who recognized her escorted her to a side entrance and up to the racing officials' executive suite.

The president of the racing association showed Angel to a seat in front of his desk; she and Chris had met him during the pre-race party the night before. Also, on hand were the association's meteorologist and the chief of the local police.

All three were falling over themselves with apologies; they'd been able to contact and recall all of the other racers—except Starr. They were continuing to try to re-establish communications, though, and assured her they'd let her know immediately once they reached him again.

But Angel just politely held up her hand.

"Chris is my boyfriend and I love him dearly," she told them. "But I'm a big girl. Please, just give it to me straight."

So they did.

True, the tsunami was thirty feet high, the race president explained, but while it wouldn't be enjoyable, most boats in its path could ride it out—all except a powerboat.

"Powerboat hulls are made of the lightest materials possible," he told her. "Any real weight it has is way back with the engines and that skews the center of gravity."

A long moment passed in silence.

"Like all powerboats, the *Temiti-Novula* is at its most seaworthy when going two hundred knots," he went on. "It was not designed to go up against gigantic waves. That's why we hold this race at this location every year.

Tidal waves are very rare in this area. The last big one they had was more than ten years ago, and that was caused by an earthquake way the hell over in Chile."

The meteorologist spoke up: "By tonight, ships of several navies will be searching a wide area west of here, looking for survivors. But truthfully, right now, our chief concern is the underwater volcano responsible for the earthquake that led to the tsunami."

"I heard something about that on the radio," Angel told him. "So, it's true?"

The men all nodded at once, grave apprehension on their faces.

"It's a new fissure out there somewhere," the weatherman said. "It's starting to erupt and that's what led to the tidal wave. No one is quite sure where the fissure is at the moment; these things are hard to detect because, even though they can be powerful, they don't make much noise and so aren't picked up very well on our tsunami detection buoys.

But if it really blows its stack, it could be very unpleasant. We'll have more earthquakes, more tsunamis. And because the water is relatively shallow in that area, we might even see an island rise out of the sea. It doesn't happen often—but if it does, then we'll have a cataclysmic volcano and that means millions of tons of ash, clouds of poison gas, fires on any land masses inside the affected zone. It will be impossible to sail into the area and very difficult to fly over it for at least twenty-four hours. So, anyone still alive out there might be in for a challenging couple days. In fact, we all will be."

"Which is why it's probably wise for you to get to someplace safe," the police chief spoke up. "Or at least away from the harbor. I can escort you personally."

Angel gracefully turned down his offer, thanked the men and left. Instead of getting away from the harbor, she pulled the beach wrap up over her head, covering her face. Then she sat on the seawall outside the race commission's headquarters away from anyone else.

Holding back the tears, she took out her Tomato Can and began pressing its power button on and off, over and over, eyes fixed on the western horizon.

"Oh, Chris . . ." she whispered. "Is there any way you got out of this?"

Chapter Four

It was the crash helmet that saved Starr's life.

He woke up on a small beach, buried in sand and debris, astonished he was still alive.

It was morning. Downed trees, clumps of palm fronds, mountains of seaweed were all around him. The *Temiti-Novula* was about 150 feet in off the beach—and about twenty feet straight up. The powerboat was wedged between two palm trees, still smoldering and doing a surreal balancing act, moving with the branches as they danced in the gentle tropical breeze.

His head hurt—but he remembered everything. One element of his STPA2 was the ability not just to recall events, but to actually *visualize* and then manipulate them in great detail. His Navy shrinks compared it to having a video playback in his head, something he could re-wind, fast forward and even stop on a mental freeze frame if he wanted to.

All he had to do was close his eyes, call up the recent happenings and they would play out for him, just like on a big TV screen.

He'd tried to outrace the tsunami—and lost.

That was the short version.

He'd turned south as soon as he saw the big wave coming at him, pushing the throttles to MOS—max operating speed—which the boat's manufacturers strongly suggested should never be employed. Now he knew why. It was like hitting the afterburner on a fighter jet. Suddenly the g-forces became even more extreme, the ocean's spray even more torrential, with his speedometer touching an astounding 250 MPH.

But tidal waves could travel more than twice that—so no matter how fast he could go, the tsunami was going to catch him.

And when it hit him, the boat would disintegrate. Light materials, screwy center of gravity, only seaworthy when going three miles a minute—Starr knew the drill, because the racing officials had explained it to him at the prerace safety briefing.

So, at that moment, his only hope was to find some kind of solid ground and try to shelter behind it. A jetty even, or maybe just some rocks. Something—anything—to spare him from the full punch of the wave's power.

And for a one brief shining moment, he thought he'd found such a place. Through the wall of unending spray, he spotted a small atoll about five miles in the distance. He immediately steered towards it, pushing his throttles up past the MOS red zone, into something called

Emergency Max, which, when activated, caused a green blinking light to appear on its read-out screen reading: "Prohibited."

A glance at the speedometer told him he'd hit 260 MPH—likely a record speed for a powerboat like this.

But then again, there was that math thing.

He and the tsunami hit the tiny island at about the same time.

The wave picked up the powerboat and sent it pin-wheeling through the air. Starr vividly replayed his being thrown from the cockpit and passing through the wave's chicane only to have what had to be the heaviest compo-nent on the boat's frame—the windshield attachment as-sembly—catch him across the right temple, a mortal blow had he not been wearing the banana-colored crash helmet.

Knocked below the crest and into the wave itself, he was carried for a couple hundred feet with the foam and the flotsam, a tremendous roar gushing in his ears, until he was finally dropped on the small beach. The rest of the wave exploded on top of him, rolling him over and over for another hundred feet until he finally came to a stop, covered in sand and detritus.

What was left of the *Temiti-Novula* went over his head a moment later. Its cockpit aflame, its engines smoking, it slammed into the two palm trees—and stayed there.

The water was lapping around his face now.

Only one eye and one nostril were above ground. Everything else was mired in the muck and debris. But he was able to hear an odd, watery whooshing sound starting to grow all around him.

He blinked away some of the sand covering his good eye to find an army of sea turtles splashing its way past him. There were dozens of them, hurrying—as fast as a turtle could—out of the sand and into the Pacific.

His first thought was that he'd suffered a concussion and was seeing things. Then one of the massive turtles came right up beside him, stopped, looked him in the eye and appeared to shake its head. Then it resumed its march to the sea.

"Now, *that* was fucked up," Starr mumbled, filling his mouth with more sand.

A moment later, he realized the water that once almost covered his face was suddenly draining away—and pulling him and all the sea turtles out with it. In seconds he was being dragged through a large, suddenly exposed oyster bed. The cracked shells were cutting his hands and feet.

He knew what was going on. Water suddenly evacuating a beach was a sure sign that another tidal wave was on its way.

Time to start moving.

He picked himself up, but took a moment to check his extremities. He could feel no broken bones, no sign of blood gushing out of him. After a quick thanks to the cosmos, he started running. Across the oyster beds, back up to the beach, under the suspended wreck of the powerboat and into the jungle.

Only after ten minutes of crashing through the thick foliage did he come to a stop. He'd reached a hill which led to a slope which led to a cliff. Five quick power breaths later, up he went, following a narrow, ancient path until he was sure he was at least fifty feet above the water line. Only then did he look back, and just in time, to see another large tidal wave smash into the island. It sounded like a freight train hitting a wall. All those tons of debris were moved another fifty feet up the beach before the wave receded again.

Starr watched it go. That made two tsunamis he'd survived already—he didn't want to try for a third.

Sweeping the sand from his bright yellow crash suit, all he had was his Tomato Can—thoroughly soaked—his pistol and his helmet. No food, no water—and absolutely no idea where he was.

His priority at that moment then was to get some idea of his location.

The path he'd been following led up past the cliff and continued to the top of a craggy summit. Its peak was where he had to be.

So he started climbing.

Chapter Five

A heavy morning mist had surrounded the atoll.

By the time Starr reached the top of the peak, it was hard to see much beyond the island itself. He would learn later that this was called the *bonne chance brouillard*—the good-luck fog.

Though the exterior was socked in, the interior was still visible through a much lighter haze. Now Starr could see the island actually had two peaks. He was on top of one; a quarter mile away, was its twin. Both were about 500 feet high; both had long cascading waterfalls plummeting from their summits. Below him was a protected, almost hidden, aqua-blue lagoon. It was a half-mile around, surrounded by pearl white beaches, mangroves and fields of tropical flowers. The heavy jungle provided such a wall around the inlet, there was only one way in and out, that was via a narrow channel at its northern end.

It was right out of a tourist brochure . . . or something. On seeing it, Starr suddenly experienced a strange wave of déjà vu. Marooned on an island. Oyster beds everywhere. Climbing to a high peak. Lots of fog. A large lagoon beneath a layer of more fog.

He felt these things had happened before—but not to him. It was as if he'd heard about them or read about them.

Strange . . .

Another odd thing—it was practically noiseless here. The ocean, now calm again, was nearly silent. The wind was no more than a light breeze, rustling only a few trees. And there were no animal noises at all.

Just very, very quiet.

Until . . .

It sounded like hammering at first. Something hard hitting something metal.

But then Starr realized the banging had a beat. Then, the smell. It was just a whiff and lasted only a second. But Starr was familiar with the aroma.

Weed . . .

Someone nearby was listening to music and getting high.

He started down a path on the other side of the peak, keeping the banging noise in front of him. The scent of marijuana became stronger with each step, leading him to a small outcrop of rock overlooking the lagoon about 250 feet down.

The fog was light enough for him to glimpse a hint of civilization below. On the western edge of the lagoon, partially hidden by a grove of palm trees, he could see the bare outlines of a camp, with people moving around it.

He continued his descent, his next stop being a ledge that looked right down on the encampment itself, now less than 150 feet away. Now he could clearly see a couple dozen individuals walking about the site.

But something was very odd here.

These people were all wearing costumes. Tri-corner hats, feathers. High black boots. Leather waist coats. Swords . . .

Pirates? he thought.

No way . . .

Then, for him, there was only one other explanation.

These people were actors.

This place was a movie set.

Starr couldn't believe his luck. Someone down there was filming a pirate movie.

Actors moving about the set. Lights everywhere. Music. Weed. A large prop cage with three damsels in distress inside. A small fleet of boats still masked by the mist out in the lagoon.

And a lot of people who looked like Johnny Depp—or Keith Richards—chipping in to clean up the location after it was just hit by the smaller but still disruptive second wave.

Then he smelled the aroma of something else: Craft Services preparing a meal; the always glamourous catering to the stars, cooking filet mignon and rice pilaf, on this little lost island.

Ah, Hollywood . . .

It had just saved him.

Or so he thought.

Chapter Six

Starr found another path that led right down to the movie set.

He took a moment to consider his next move. Approach, but stealthily. Ask to get word back to Papeete, but not with a lot of details. As for who he was, in his bright yellow safety suit and helmet, he'd have no trouble selling his cover story as a powerboat driver.

He hid his pistol in his boot and stuffed the Tomato Can in his thigh pocket. The old sat-phone was ruined, but it was still classified technology and there was no way he could just toss it away. But he didn't want anyone else getting a look at it.

He buttoned the pocket, took five easy breaths this time, and started down the path, ready to make some new friends.

But suddenly his STPA2 kicked in . . .

Duck . . . now!

The fist came out of nowhere. It just missed catching him on the right temple, the same side where he'd already banged his melon. He successfully dodged the unseen assailant's right cross, but wasn't so lucky with the follow-up left hook.

Despite his trusty crash helmet, that punch dropped him like a rock.

When his wits finally returned, he was looking up at a very attractive blonde. Short clipped hair, enormous blue eyes, she was dressed in skimpy shorts and a tight t-shirt. She was looking down at him with concern on her, yes, *camouflaged*, face.

Through the sound of a million bees buzzing around his head, he heard her say: "Fuck me dead. Thank God—you're alive!"

In the next moment, she was on top of him, one knee in his crotch, a large knife at his throat.

"What are you doing here?" she hissed. "Are you with them?"

The bees were still in his head, but Starr was aware enough to know the woman was probably not part of a movie crew, but rather a military unit. It was not just her camouflage war paint, which looked to have been applied by expert hands, but also the way she moved. Quiet, cautious, but aggressive.

Time to break cover.

"I'm U.S. Navy," he groaned.

She laughed, her knife pressing closer to his neck.

"Of course, you are," she replied. "Look at the way you're dressed. You're a god-damned banana."

Starr might have laughed if his jaw didn't hurt so much. Luckily he had one thing to prove who he was. Moving very slowly, he pulled out the Tomato Can, drew back its well-conceived false cover to reveal a very high-tech, if elderly satellite phone within.

It was water-logged, but his ID, name and ONI serial number could still be seen on the fogged-over sign-off screen. It had just enough James-Bondness for his ac-coster to give him a second look.

"I'm U.S. Navy Intelligence," he told her, getting his full voice back. "I'm on a case."

Convinced, she withdrew her knife and helped him up.

He brushed himself off and said. "OK—your turn?"

"First Sergeant Ozzie Gull," she told him, shaking his hand. "Her Majesty's Seventh Regiment, Australian Special Forces."

As it turned out, Starr had it all wrong.

The men walking around the camp were not actors. The damsels in the cage were not actresses.

Their jail cell was not a prop; it was a repurposed shark cage. The two men standing guard in front of it were armed with real weapons.

"But why are they all wearing pirate outfits?" Starr whispered to Sergeant Oz.

"Because they *are* pirates," she whispered back. "They're either meth heads or they've been watching too many movies. Or both. But they *are* pirates. They landed here the day after we did. And we even know why they are here . . ."

Starr and Oz were in a "double-S Opie"—an SAS-style, sub-surface observation post. It was five feet deep counting the half foot of turf on top, and flush with the side of a hill that looked right into the pirates' camp not 30 feet away. Oz had told him it had been a bitch to con-struct—and Starr could tell. Though it had been dug into the sand, some of the roots that had been cut through were a foot or more around. Still the place was almost roomy, with a step-up to a slit-like aperture, giving an almost panoramic view of the lagoon. Yet, from the out-side, the Opie was so expertly camouflaged, it was liter-ally invisible to the pirates.

The three women in the cage were the other members of Oz's SF group, known as 4Team. They were on the island conducting what the Australian military called an EMS—an extreme measures survival exercise.

Dropped here for twenty-one days, with no provi-sions, no communications gear, just knives, their sparse utility outfits and their wits, their mission had two parts. Survive in the wild and live under concealment. The team had planned to build as many as a dozen double-S Opies on the island during their three weeks here.

Then the first wave hit.

Standing on the Opie's observers' step, looking out the slit opening into the pirate camp and beyond now, Oz directed Starr's attention to a beach on the far side of the lagoon and a small mountain of oyster shells gleaming in the morning sun.

"*That's* why these guys are here," she told him.

"To steal oysters?"

"Not the oysters," she replied, straight-faced, her Australian accent curling every other syllable. "The pearls. The people in the area call this island Amatupu. Its oyster beds are enormous, especially in that lagoon. But they are part of a sheltered environmental trust. The proceeds from any pearls harvested here go to orphanages throughout Polynesia. These guys are literally taking food from the mouths of motherless babes."

She explained her three teammates had been captured during the chaos after the first tsunami hit the island. In fact, the trio had been in this very same OP when the wave arrived.

"The pirates are somewhat protected here," Oz said. "The edge of lagoon, with lots of jungle and two small mountains in between. But the tsunami still swamped this place. It hit so unexpectedly, a bunch of the pirates were swept away in the first few seconds. I was back at our bivouac for resupply when it happened, but I know my soldiers. I know they made the decision on their own to help some of the other pirates who'd been caught in the surge and were in danger of drowning. They must have broken cover to save them."

But the humanitarian act backfired. Oz saw the three unit members captured a short time later, putting her team in this very sticky position. Their presence on the uncharted island was supposed to be a secret. But now, at the very least, they'd compromised their mission.

"Ever think this might be part of your training?" Starr asked her in another whisper.

"My bosses don't have any sense of humor," she told him dryly, not even cracking a grin. "They wouldn't have sent these poofs if it was part of a drill."

She paused a moment, then added: "Besides, as bad as all this looks, it might not be our biggest problem . . ."

No sooner had she said those words when the ground started shaking.

"Damn," she hissed. "Not again . . ."

She pulled him off the step and to the floor of the OP. They sat there, together, while the earth shook for almost a minute.

Starr felt every muscle in his body tense up and stay that way, Angel's words flashing back to him many times in those sixty seconds. He'd never been in an earthquake before. For him, too, it was the longest minute in his life.

Then, just as abruptly, everything stopped shaking. But Starr and Oz didn't move; they didn't speak.

The tremor had disrupted the pirates' base nearby. Shouting, confusion, unexpected disarray for the third time in less than a day.

Using the din from the camp to cover their movements, Oz pushed Starr out the rear entrance of the OP and together, they disappeared back into the jungle.

Chapter Seven

They were called M2G, abbreviated from the Maru-Maru Gang.

And they *were* indeed real pirates.

But they were also murderers and rapists.

The damage to their camp on the edge of the lagoon would be significant but manageable. The big tremor came just as the gang had finished scooping up thousands of oyster shells from the lagoon. It tipped over a few of their hootches, destroyed half of the fresh water supply and, once again, gave their goats conniptions.

But once the initial chaos died down, the gang went back to business as usual.

They'd started in 2013 in a prison near the Indonesian city of Palu. Twenty of the two dozen original members were in jail there for homicide or sexual assault.

In early October of 2018, Palu was hit by . . . an earthquake and then a tsunami. In the pandemonium that followed, M2G, along with 400 other inmates, broke down the main doors of the prison and escaped.

The gang looted a fishing village nearby, killing dozens and stealing three 70-foot fishing boats. They sailed east, fleeing Indonesian authorities, eventually winding up in the warm, lucrative waters of French Polynesia, 7,000 miles away.

They became pirates not from any ancestral calling or seafaring DNA in their veins. M2G were simply big fans of pirate films; they'd devoted much time in prison watching the adventures of Jake Sparrow, over and over, memorizing lines and reciting them in unison along with the movies. Once free, the gang began accumulating the costumes they liked in those films, the more flamboyant, the better.

Now the wild regalia was their brand, known to all throughout Polynesia, including the *Gendarmerie*, the French national police force responsible for law enforcement in the islands.

While their criminal activity consisted mostly of raiding isolated villages and robbing luxury yachts in the waters around Tahiti, M2G also came here frequently, to the western edge of the Leewards, to rape the Amatupu oyster beds and steal their priceless pearls.

They'd arrived a few days before the first tsunami hit, setting up in one of their several camps on the island. Like everyone else, the two tidal waves took them by surprise. The first one arrived so unexpectedly, a half-dozen gang members were swept away by the surge, a blow to the 30-member crew as it meant there would be less people to harvest the pearls.

But M2G had experience riding out natural disasters and the aftermath of the first wave provided them with an unexpected bonus: Having the three young females fall into their laps was like a miracle to them. The girls claimed to be contestants trying out for a new Australian reality show when they rescued six other gang members from the tsunami. It had been heartwarming and heroic, but whatever the case, it was their bad luck.

M2G didn't meet many women in their travels. Those they did rarely lived to tell about it.

So, when it came to their latest guests, it wasn't a matter of if, but of when . . . and how.

Twenty minutes after the sixty-second tremor, Oz and Starr arrived at 4Team's main bivouac, their base of operations.

It was an expanded version of the Opie near the pirate base. A large, rectangular pit built flush into the side of a mountain, complete with turf roof, twenty feet from a rocky beach, about a mile south from where Starr washed up.

It was in a perfect location and was another master-work of camouflage. An almost panoramic view of the entire eastern edge of the island, while still hidden in the flora and being high enough to survive surges resulting from two tsunamis.

But the place was noticeably empty. The bare provisions of Oz's captured colleagues were conspicuously piled in one corner.

"Sorry, we don't have any coffee," she told him once they were inside. "Or tea . . ."

"Not a problem," he replied. "How many of those tremors have you felt?"

"In the six days we've been here, at least a dozen," she replied digging in her rucksack for something. "But that one was the strongest yet."

"Two tidal waves and six shocks," Starr said. "You're sure getting a lot of experience in these things—whatever these things are . . ."

She finally found what she was looking for. A pack of bubble gum.

"My only luxury," she said sheepishly.

She took out a stick, tore it neatly in half and passed one piece to him.

"Earthquakes and tsunamis aren't all," she went on. "There's been some very strange things happening here in the past few days."

"Stranger than running into a gang of Johnny Depp impersonators?"

She almost smiled, her camouflage paint starting to run with sweat.

"Two nights ago, we heard this crazy rustling in the jungle," she began. "It sounded like a herd of elephants. Turned out to be thousands of snakes, slithering through the forest and heading into the sea. And I mean *thousands* of them.

"Then the next morning, all the frogs were doing the same thing. For as far as we could see up and down the beach, thousands of frogs jumping in the ocean."

Starr told her about the march of turtles he'd witnessed after he arrived.

"Animals sense these things," she said, popping her half-piece of gum into her mouth. "And just listen . . . hear anything?"

Starr shook his head no. As before the island seemed eerily quiet.

"No birds," she said. "When we got here, they never shut up. Now there's nothing. They all left too. That might be the weirdest thing of all. This freaking quiet."

They sat silently for a moment, chewing their bubble gum.

"I'll be honest with you, lieutenant," she said to him, unconsciously blowing a large pink bubble. "I'm so afraid to think what's coming next I'm ready to bugger the exercise, get my people back and get off this rock."

"I'm with you, sergeant," Starr replied. "I just wish I had a way of doing just that. I guess if this was a real movie, we'd construct a boat out of coconut trees and be gone in a day. I'm in the Navy—but I don't have the slightest idea about how to build a boat."

She thought a moment and then began reapplying some of her running camo face paint.

"Is there any chance you're a pilot, then?" she asked.

An unusual question to ask.

"I know how to fly," he replied. "Why?"

Chapter Eight

Five minutes later Starr was climbing again.

Following on Oz's heels, they went up and down the first peak again, and then crossed a precarious land bridge made of slate and old oyster shells leading to the second peak.

After ascending that summit and going down its other side, there came thirty minutes of moving through even thicker jungle before they finally reached the southern tip of the island.

There were no pearl-white beaches here. It was a coastal plateau, flat and covered with well-trimmed grass. Maybe 250 feet above the ocean and at least twice that wide, it was bordered by vividly colored tropical plants with columns of rainbow-crested waves crashing dramatically on its rocks below.

There was no fog here either. The crystal-clear Pacific was sparkling in the mid-morning sun and the view was spectacular. For the first time, Starr could see other islands scattered about in the distance.

The beauty of this place went beyond what any tourist brochure could ever convey. Starr didn't believe in magic—not exactly anyway. But he could see why someone might call this place magical.

No sooner did that thought go through his head, when another wave of the strange déjà vu came over him. This place was familiar somehow, or he'd been told about it, or had read about it. He couldn't put his finger on it. A displaced memory, it was impossible to shake.

They didn't speak much during their journey here. Just as she'd requested, they'd moved through the jungle as quickly and silently as possible. Now crouched on the edge of the green grass lawn, they shared another stick of bubble gum.

"We found this place our first day out," she told him. "During our preliminary reconnoiter. It was a bit of a surprise, I can say . . ."

"I'm not trying to be funny," Starr replied, still taking in the place. "But it really looks like something from a movie."

She almost smiled at that.

"You haven't seen anything yet," she said.

They made their way across the plateau, hidden by the last of the morning shadows.

Starr was surprised to see there were two buildings up here. Camouflaged not by human hands, but by time and nature, both were hidden beneath enormous trees dangling long strands of what looked like weeping willow branches, but covered with bright pink flowers.

One building was an old French Polynesian plantation mansion. Faded sun-bleached white, it had three levels with lots of windows and teak-wood balconies, now entwined with the tumbling flowered branches.

The other structure was clearly an aircraft hangar.

"I wish I'd landed on this part of the island," Starr said, looking at the mansion. "I wouldn't mind moving into that place for a while."

"Maybe, maybe not," Oz replied, adding: "Listen again for a moment. What do you hear?"

As before, Starr heard nothing. No animal sounds. No birds.

But then—a man's voice.

Crying out? No, shouting instructions to somebody. The same thing, over and over.

It was coming from inside the mansion. But there was something off about the voice.

"Recorded?" he asked her.

She nodded and said: "It gets even better."

She brought him around to the rear of the mansion to the servants' entrance. Using her survival knife to pick the door's lock, they went in, being careful to shut the door behind them. He followed her through an elaborate, vintage kitchen to a small bedroom attached to the pantry.

There was a figure lying on the bed, dressed in what looked like an old NASA astronaut's spacesuit, shiny like aluminum foil. But its owner was long dead; a skeleton was all that remained, a pistol still in his bony hand, still pointing at his right temple.

On the table next to the bed was a smartphone, which in turn was attached to a small solar panel sitting on the windowsill. The phone's PLAY button was being held down with a rubber band and it appeared to operate only when enough solar power had been gathered to charge the battery and play a recorded message.

But what was it?

On cue, the phone started buzzing again.

"Jake!" the voice bellowed. "Stay off the god-damn bed!"

Starr looked at Oz. "Jake?"

She motioned him to the other side of the room where he saw another skeleton. This one was of a large dog that had expired curled up on the floor next to the bed, heeding his master's final command into eternity.

Starr was bewildered. The NASA suit? The phone message? The dead dog? Again, he looked to Oz, hoping for some kind of explanation.

But she could only shake her head.

"All we found was this," she told him, passing him a note that was on the room's bureau. "It looks like it's been here for at least a few months."

Written with a shaky hand, the note read: *I'm sorry. I didn't want to leave like this, but I couldn't take the ground shaking anymore. The noise drove me crazy.*

They left the scene intact, closing and locking all the doors behind them. The cell's battery would eventually wear out and recharging it would become impossible. Ingenious as it was, the system would then break down and die a slow death.

But there was no reason for them to disturb anything.

They moved on to the hangar.

It too was both regal and quaint, old but well-built of teak and red clay. Two huge doors on rollers fronted the place, a rusty but still-working lock held them together.

"Any idea what's in here?" he asked her, taking a measure of the place.

"We had a quick peek," she replied.

Once again she used the tip of her survival knife to pick the lock. Then she rolled the doors back to reveal a very old, very unusual airplane.

It was a Mosquito, a two-propeller British-designed attack plane from World War Two. Bigger than a fighter, but smaller than a bomber, it was all curves and flares, with not a right angle in sight. A beautiful design, it looked fast even while standing still.

Mosquitoes were famous for two things: because of steel shortages in the UK during the war, the British built them almost entirely out of wood. Second, because the British then put two gigantic Rolls Royce engines on them, for most of the conflict, this wooden airplane could outrun anything in the sky. Mosquitoes could go so fast—nearly 420 MPH—some reconnaissance versions didn't even carry weapons. They would simply hit the gas and wave goodbye to anyone chasing them.

But this particular Mosquito was not unarmed. Starr recognized the model as a Mark 18, a combined fighter-bomber version of the legendary airplane. It still had the speed—but it also carried a massive 57-millimeter anti-tank gun inside. The muzzle of this nine-foot monster stuck out under the airplane's nose and, like an artillery piece with wings, could fire massive high-explosive shells weighing nearly ten pounds each.

One shot from this aerial cannon could sink a submarine. Two could break a destroyer in half. A half dozen hits or more and the target would be obliterated. The weapon was so fierce the Mosquito's nose also carried four Browning 50-caliber machine guns, but only to help the pilot aim his much bigger gun.

For Starr, it was like looking at a vintage race car. The engines were spotless; the blue camo paint smelled fresh. The big cannon and its attendant four machine guns were loaded, racks greased, barrels clean—all the more amazing in this tropical environment. Someone had been keeping the airplane in top shape for a long time.

So, was the dead man in the house the owner . . . or the caretaker? Either way, the plane had been beautifully preserved. Whoever it belonged to had to be a collector.

"Can you fly it?" Oz asked him. "Can you get us all off this rock?"

Starr hesitated answering for a moment. He'd taken jet fighter training before the Navy transferred him to NILE. He'd done carrier landings, day and night, plus he'd flown a number of different airframes in his present assignment as a naval investigator.

But walking back out onto the bluff and looking at the ocean below, he knew getting airborne under these conditions would not be easy. Take off would basically mean gunning the engines, going off the cliff and hoping enough air got under the wings before you fell into the sea. Landing would be just as treacherous, accomplished by way of a tail hook assembly attached to the rear of the plane. Three wires were stretched across the grass runway at the far end of the plateau. The Mosquito would have to get this rear hook to snag one of the three wires on landing, pulling the plane to a stop. Miss the wires and you were definitely going for a swim.

"I can *try* to fly it," was how he finally answered. "But this plane was built for two. With five on board, it might get interesting."

She understood, but then said: "Well, I've got to get them back first."

He turned around and looked at her. She was pretty under all the camo face paint.

"*We've* got to get them back," he told her matter-of-factly. "I'm going to help you."

That's when she finally smiled—and she immediately went from pretty to beautiful.

She reached out to touch his arm, to thank him—when suddenly the ground started shaking again.

It was much more violent this time. Everything around them began swaying back and forth, up and down.

Then, looking across the ocean directly in front of them, maybe fifteen miles to the west, a plume of white smoke suddenly exploded out of the water. It went up more than a mile in just seconds, like water spewing from a gigantic fire hose. Starr had never seen anything like it.

But Oz had.

"That's an underwater volcano," she gasped. "The tsunamis, the earthquakes, the animals leaving—everything. *This* is why . . ."

The ash plume grew quickly, forming itself into a grotesque, misshapen mushroom cloud with flashes of lightning crackling within. The sky around it turned bright orange; thunderclaps echoed into the heavens. Then huge huffs of lava appeared, cooled and started to form land—all right before their eyes. There was a bizarre beauty to it.

But at the same time, they could see projectiles being ejected from the hellish scene, leaving fiery trails behind them. Quick calculations told Starr these missiles were as big as houses and at least a half dozen of them were heading right for the island, followed by a storm of hot ash, gas and dust, all mixed together.

Only then did the noise finally hit . . .

It shredded Starr's eardrums—he could feel the sonics stretching the skin of his face. It made what he'd felt at 200 knots on the powerboat seem like a mild breeze.

They acted quickly. Starr pulled Oz back into the hangar and rolled the doors shut. Then they both scrambled under the wing of the Mosquito and closed up as tight as they could.

The noise outside grew to a high-pitched scream. Starr put his arm around her. She got as close to him as possible.

Then everything went black.

Chapter Nine

It seemed to go on forever.

The noise. The wind. The heat. The ground rumbling mightily. Starr and Oz didn't move, trying their best to stay hunkered down and keep it together while the world was going crazy outside.

Ten minutes went by. Fifteen. Twenty . . .

Then, suddenly, everything just stopped. A terrible silence descended on the island. They remained frozen in place.

It was still pitch black inside the hangar. What looked like a fine dirty snow was falling in between the cracks in the roof and blowing in from under the air barn's doors.

This was ash from the volcano. The problem was it would continue to accumulate, fouling the air to the point that it would begin choking them to death. Outside, it would be worse.

This was getting serious. As a kid, Starr had flown over what was left of Mount St. Helens and the sight of the devastation never left him. Hundreds of square miles had been blanketed with the suffocating slag, most of it falling in the first few minutes of the eruption and killing everything underneath.

Oz, on the other hand, was furious that they'd been caught in this spot.

"Oh, my God," she spit angrily. "What a way to go, really?"

Starr couldn't disagree. This was how many people died in volcanic eruptions, not from the lava or the blast itself, but from asphyxiation.

They both began coughing. With each breath, they took in more of the ash-tainted air, making them cough even more.

The situation became so desperate, so quickly, Starr expected his life to flash before his eyes.

Instead, his ESP suddenly kicked in.

Oxygen . . .

He was up on the Mosquito's wing in seconds, crawling across to the cockpit, and not quite believing what he found secured between the pilots' seats: two portable oxygen tanks with masks attached. It was the air crew's emergency supply. The old aircraft had been that well-maintained—every last item in working condition and in its place.

"Whoever that spaceman laying in there is," Starr told her, handing down one of the tanks and mask, then taking the other set himself. "We owe him big time . . ."

They put on their masks and started the oxygen flowing. The tanks were about the size of a liter bottle, not too heavy, but awkward to carry. They both took a hefty gulp of oxygen, then rolled back the hangar's doors and stumbled outside.

It was dark as night. One huge black cumulus cloud stretched to every horizon, dispensing a blizzard of dirty snow on everything beneath.

Starr felt like he'd woken up in the middle of a familiar childhood nightmare. He'd had it a few times growing up. One moment, the sun is out, and it's almost midday. Then something happens and suddenly its nighttime, it's dark out and you don't know why.

The world around them had turned a sickly gray. The once beautiful flowers, the bluff itself, even the ocean—everything was covered in ash. Behind them, a large part of the jungle was smoldering. At least a few of the projectiles they'd seen launched from the volcano had come down on the island like meteors, gashing huge holes in the forest not far away.

This place didn't look so magical anymore. Now it looked like the set of an f/x-heavy horror movie.

They each checked the other's oxygen mask and then started running. Through the jungle, up and down the southern peak, across the land bridge and down towards the lagoon, every step was slippery. The sooty ash was almost a foot deep in some places, making it difficult to move, never mind run.

Still, they made it back to the other side of the island in a very short time, sucking heavily on their oxygen tanks the whole way. By this time, the winds had picked up and had blown a lot of the deadly ash back out to sea. Still, the sickly gray snowflakes continued to fall.

They made their way down to the observation post looking out on the pirates' base.

Or where the base used to be.

Because the little inlet off the lagoon where the pirates had been camped was now empty.

The lights, the shark cage, the oysters, the three fishing boats—and the trio of Oz's captured soldiers—were all gone.

Chapter Ten

The Maui-Maui Gang had learned a lot about the islands of far western Polynesia since coming here.

Many featured expansive lagoons guarded by soaring peaks. Most of them had thick jungles and were overgrown with exotic flowers. Most, like Amatupu, were uninhabited.

This island also had an interesting feature on its southwestern side. It was a deep, but narrow channel which ran in from the sea, passing beneath a high, sheer, vine-covered cliff.

Once through these overhanging branches, the channel led to a hidden cove, impossible to see except from the air, and then someone would have to be looking for it, as it too was surrounded by clumps of overgrown and inter-tangled vegetation.

This was where the pirates went after pilfering the island's oyster fields because it was a better hiding place.

The hidden cove was just big enough to fit their three ships. As a bonus, there were a number of caves located on the side of the sheer cliff, plus the winds were constant and favorable here. While the air was still filled with some falling ash, breathing was not such a chore as on other parts of the island.

Nevertheless, the pirates took generators and large drying fans from their ships and set them up at the mouth of the largest cave opening, about fifty feet up from the sea, straddling both the channel and the hidden cove.

The fans served to blow the tainted air back out the opening while drawing up the fresher air from deep in the cave itself.

But as a cruel safety check, to make sure the air they were breathing wasn't deadly, the pirates placed the shark cage prison with their three captives at the front of the cave. Like canaries in a coal mine, if the women started having breathing problems, that would tell the gang members to take action and move deeper into the cave.

Only the long-term veterans of the gang were afforded this luxury. After sealing off their three ships by duct taping all of the portholes and doorways and running their air circulation systems on high, the junior rank pirates would spend the night shucking the thousands of oysters stolen from the lagoon and retrieving the valuable pearls inside.

There was one big advantage connected to this work. The junior pirates could eat all the oysters they wanted, in preparation for the blowout they expected to have once the shucking was complete and the three female captives were made available to them to do with whatever they wanted.

The pirates had arrived at the hidden cove base in the afternoon, about an hour after the underwater eruption shook the island from one end to the other.

They knew that search and rescue airplanes would start to appear over the area soon. That there was still some smoke and ash still blowing around worked to the pirates' advantage in at least one respect: it would obscure any infrared instruments that might be looking down on the island.

Besides, the new piece of dry earth emerging from the ocean just fifteen miles away was going to be the main attraction in these parts for the next twenty-four hours or more.

They would be well hidden inside the cove for at least that long.

Or so they thought.

As the afternoon turned into evening and evening into night, the eerie quiet of the strange little island was violated every so often by the sound of an airplane flying overhead, above the ash cloud, coming or going from the smoldering volcano.

This was either a media aircraft or one laden with scientific instruments, and the pirates had expected it, being around disaster sites before.

What they didn't expect to hear was another airplane, flying much lower, much closer, much faster and making much more noise.

And it was looking for something. It was easy to tell, because whenever they heard it, the engine sound would come and go, indicating the plane was flying a typical grid-like search pattern. Sometimes getting very close to the hidden cove before flying away again, in the dark hours after midnight, the disturbing mechanical drone was never far away.

High pitched. Mechanical.

Not a jet, but something that just sounded *fast*.

It got so troubling that around 2 a.m., the pirates turned off all their fans and all machinery running in their ships and the cave, attempting to go completely silent and hoping the plane would go away, and stay away.

But it didn't. They heard it all night long. It not only kept them awake, it disrupted the shucking operation, because they needed to run their ships' generators to have the light to retrieve the pearls.

No power, no light, no pearls.

***

Morning arrived.

The *bonne chance brouillard* appeared on schedule, the thick early ring of mist collaring the island and concealing the channel, the cliffs, the caves, the hidden cove and the pirates' ships. The ash hadn't stopped falling; it was still in the air, but it was little more than constant flurry of the black snow, blowing in the wind.

But the dawn also brought relief.

Just as the last of the stars were winking out, the noise of the mystery plane finally went away. The pirates could hear waves crashing all around the island and the occasional rumble from the nearby volcano—but that was it.

With the air somewhat breathable now, the shipbound pirates uncovered their portholes, turned on their generators and resumed the shucking operation.

Meanwhile the senior pirates dared to venture out of the cave, making their way down to the hidden cove. Setting up several oil can fires, they began frying rumsoaked mangoes on a large grill, beginning their morning meal.

The word from the three ships floating in a triangle pattern nearby was that the pearl harvest was already enormous, with the shucking operation still an hour away from completion.

This was a reason to celebrate. The blowout, the rave they'd been planning, with their prisoners as special guests, would begin the moment the last oyster was shucked, the last pearl stolen.

The mangoes were eaten, more rum and coffee were poured. Sitting on the edge of the hidden cove, the gang was able to relax for the first time in almost two days. But not for long—because just as the pirates began lighting up their morning pot blunts—another ritual—terror struck from the sky.

At first a lot of the pirates thought it was some sort of flying creature. Huge and dark, it came out of the ash and fog so quickly, it just didn't seem real. There was a very rare bird seen in these islands called the Rondan, a giant, almost-prehistoric animal of prey. For many of the pirates, *this* is what they saw.

But others saw a warplane—one with a very large gun sticking out of its nose.

That gun fired once. The flash was blinding, the recoil so powerful it seemed like the aircraft stood still for a moment, before dashing away. At the same moment, one of the three pirate ships blew up, the aerial shell penetrating its hull and igniting its fuel supply.

The ship broke in half and sank in the deep waters of the hidden cove, all in about ten seconds.

The pirates could hear the ghost plane go into a steep climb right over their heads, its engines screaming, only to turn over and come back down again.

The pirates scattered. As before, the airplane came out of the murk, flying above the channel and parallel to the opening of the pirate's cave. Once again it fired a single massive shell. Blinding flash, a stop-action moment for the warplane—and then a second ship was rocked by an explosion.

In less than a minute, this ship joined its companion sinking into the bottomless cove.

The two pirates in charge of guarding the three prisoners in the shark cage didn't know what to do.

They'd watched the whole drama from their elevated perch up the bluff, next to the cave opening, looking down on the hidden cove.

Something had gone terribly wrong. The attacking airplane had flown so close to their position, they could see the pilot looking over at them as he zoomed by. Now, two of their ships had been sunk inside the cove without so much as a bubble, and the crew of the third was trying desperately to turn around and attempt an escape to the sea.

In the middle of this confusion, the two guards saw something that just didn't seem real to them. There were shrubs and trees and vines growing all around the cave's opening. The flora helped hide the entrance.

Suddenly a section of this natural camouflage came to life and started walking towards them. They were completely baffled as to what was going on. They raised their weapons, ready to blast away at it, but two flashes of light emerged from the tree and both pirates dropped to the ground, a bullet to each skull.

At that moment, the strange airplane roared by a third time, much louder and much lower. It went right by the cave opening, once again firing its massive internal weapon. Two more shots and the third ship sank in just a few seconds.

Oz quickly threw off her camouflaged gown and picked the lock on the shark cage. Her three teammates were shocked to see her, and *very* shocked that they were suddenly free.

She gave them just one order: "Follow me—double time."

Chapter Eleven

It took the four members of 4Team less than 20 minutes to reach the island's southern side plateau.

They arrived just in time to see the Mosquito almost crash.

The ash had stopped falling; the plateau looked like it was covered with six inches of very dirty snow, the wind twisting some of it into mini-tornadoes.

The Mosquito was circling the bluff, at once coming down very low, going very fast, only to pull up and climb again.

It took a few moments for Oz to realize what Starr was doing.

Then, it hit her.

She ordered her unit forward. They ran across the plateau and uncovered the three arresting wires from the ash. Fallen palm fronds worked the best as brooms. The Mosquito circled the plateau twice more and came down, the arresting cables being as clean as they were ever going to be.

The noise was tremendous, a high-pitched cry of two aircraft engines echoed across the plateau as the Mosquito's tail hook just barely snagged the third and last arresting wire.

The plane slammed into the blanket of ash, kicking up so much with its impact along with the backwash of the two powerful engines, 4Team lost sight of it.

But not its noise.

When the cloud of ash cleared, they saw that Starr had turned the plane around into a take-off profile and was hanging out of the cockpit's open window, beckoning them to get on board.

Oz helped them up the under-fuselage entry way. At Starr's direction, the first soldier lay down on the floor at the back of the already cramped cabin in an attempt to equalize the weight in the already dangerously overloaded aircraft.

The second soldier strapped into the navigators seat; the third team member sat on her lap. With absolutely no room left, Sergeant Oz would wind up on Starr's lap. But just as she was about to climb aboard, there was a tremendous *bang!* and the entire island began violently shaking again.

Fifteen miles away, across the dirty blue sea, the volcano was erupting once more.

Oz climbed into the plane and secured the cockpit hatch.

Starr took a quick look around the cabin—and felt the odd déjà vu wash over him again. A dangerously overloaded airplane? Trying to take off from a cliff?

Why did this all seem so damn familiar?

He turned the Mosquito around one more time, pointing the nose of the vintage aircraft towards the sea—and the erupting volcano.

Again, just as he'd done once before, he would have to get the engines revved as high as possible then drive off the cliff—and hope the damn thing would fly despite all the extra weight he was carrying.

He crossed his fingers—sent a quick message to the cosmos—then popped the plane's brakes.

But then something *really* strange happened.

As they were rumbling across the plateau and the ash was blowing like stirred-up snow, Starr just happened to glance out the cockpit window to his left and for a moment thought he saw a crowd of people there, waving goodbye to him, some with tiny American flags.

Then he blinked—and the vision was gone.

Chapter Twelve

The Mosquito went off the side of the cliff—and started plunging immediately.

They were 300 pounds overweight—and with this moment of terror, they were suddenly paying the price.

Starr made a quick decision. Even as the waves were coming up to meet them, he booted the power and then went hard right.

Again, the beauty of the Mosquito was it was made of wood and carried two giant engines. Like a light-weight race car with an enormous motor, the plane quickly obeyed and went right—hard. Everyone on board went with it, almost crushed by the sudden on-slaught of g-forces.

When Starr opened his eyes again, they were flying somewhat sideways, but climbing.

It was another ten seconds of their lives that they would never forget. The Mosquito was so fast, it was al-most like riding in a jet—and it was that speed that saved them from the drink.

It took Starr two more minutes to get complete con-trol of the overloaded and unbalanced aircraft. But fi-nally at 5,000 feet, he was able to turn back over the island and climb above the explosion of ash and hot gases as it came rolling across the water, hitting the island like a tsunami of smoke.

Starr leveled off, more than a mile above the tiny island—it was the first and probably last time he'd have the opportunity to see it from this height, this angle.

It turned out to be a strange perspective—and an unexpected one. For the first time, Starr realized the island was actually heart-shaped.

And that seemed familiar to him too.

He turned the old plane southeast, towards Tahiti, while Sergeant Oz, still ensconced on his lap, tried to get the radio to work. If everything stayed the same, they could be in Papeete in less than an hour. If the plane's radio actually worked, they could contact the Tahitian capital, and ask that someone get a message to Angel that he was OK.

For the first time in a long time, he was able to exhale and take into account what had just happened. It all went by so quickly, but at the same time, it seemed to last forever.

His would not be the first or the last special ops mission that became sidetracked. It was the nature of a business that was highly unpredictable.

They'd busted up a pretty nasty gang of sea-faring murderers and they'd seen a new land mass be formed. Not quite mission accomplished, but . . .

Suddenly, the voice inside him—the one he always considered the mouthpiece for his STPA2—was telling him to go back—go back to the island.

"Why?" Oz asked him once she realized what was happening.

"Because something just isn't right," Starr replied.

He didn't need his ESP to figure out why he'd been pulled back to the island.

As he banked to the right, he found himself looking down on the northeast edge of the atoll—not far from where he'd been shipwrecked.

And below him were two ships.

One looked like a research ship; the other was a military vessel. Both were flying a red flag festooned with yellow stars.

Chinese . . .

Starr could see a small army of people in hazmat suits marching up the beach—and heading right for the grove of palm trees where his powerboat had jammed itself, what seemed like a million years ago.

The Chinese were here, intent on fulfilling their mission.

That's why Starr had to fulfill his first.

But how—without starting World War Three?

He told everyone on board to get secured.

Then he armed the big anti-tank gun, went into a dive and zeroed in on his target—the remains of the massive powerboat still hanging in the trees, its pair of XB-44 engines still attached.

One shell would have done it. But he fired three times and wiped out not just the remains of the powerboat, but the entire grove of palm trees around it.

Starr then put the Mosquito into a tight 180-degree turn and flew over the beach where the Chinese thieves were now just reacting to the powerboat blowing up. They scattered as he flew very low right over their heads.

Another turn to the left and he buzzed both ships waiting off shore.

Then he climbed and didn't stop until he was nearly 10-angels. Two miles up.

They all looked back down at the heart-shaped island wrapped in the good luck fog once again.

"Strange place . . ." Oz said, readjusting herself on his lap.

"The strangest," he agreed.

It took a few minutes, but finally Oz managed to coax the old radio back to life. She was soon talking to the Royal Australian Air Force on their emergency radio frequency.

It was a brief conversation. Oz almost laughed and directed their attention towards their three o'clock position. Out of the clouds, two RAAF F-18 fighters suddenly appeared.

"They were dispatched this morning to look for us," Oz told those on board.

Starr started wagging his wings. "Well, they found us," he said. Looking around the vintage cockpit and out on the camo-blue, WW2 style wings, he added: "We're hard to miss, I guess."

The fighter pilots rocketed by the Mosquito, then went into wide turns and came back up on them, forming an escort.

Flying very slow as the Mosquito was flying very fast, One of the F-18s were soon right beside them. Seeing Starr driving the plane with one female on his lap and others crowded inside the cabin, the Aussie pilot gave him an enthusiastic thumbs-up, then a salute and then pulled back into the escort formation.

A moment later, Starr felt a jolt of electricity go through his body. His STPA2 was kicking in. He was suddenly close to euphoric.

The Tomato Can rang an instant later, suddenly working again. But he knew it was going to happen. He also knew it could only be one person . . .

"Angel?" he whispered into the sat-phone.

"My God, Chris—you're there? You're OK?"

She was crying and laughing at the same time.

"I'm good," he told her. "Everything still works. How are you?"

"This place is still recovering from the earthquake," she said. "But the power is back on and everything has opened back up."

"That's great to hear," he replied. "So please reserve us a couple chairs on the beach and maybe some bubbly or something. I'll be there in about two hours."

Now she was mostly laughing; everything was OK.

"You're sure you're all right?" she asked him.

He looked around the cabin of the old plane, the four beauties, the World War Two instrument panels, the enormous anti-gun which ran right through the lower cabin, and then the two RAAF fighter jets riding alongside them.

"Just a typical day, honey," he said. "See you soon . . ."

Book Three

<u>The Haunted Saddle</u>

Chapter One

Somewhere over the Pacific

Admiral Hawley had never flown on a CIA airplane before.

He'd served in the ONI for 22 years and worked with the Agency on at least a dozen cases. But this was the first time they'd ever given him a lift.

He was heading for Hawaii, the only passenger on the flight. An emergency security briefing had been called for later that day at U.S. Navy Fleet Headquarters in Pearl Harbor. The meeting was so top secret only a handful of people in Washington DC were even aware of it.

Though Hawley had left San Diego just 90 minutes before, he was already halfway to his destination. The CIA plane was a new Gulfstream G-602 business jet—at least outwardly. But once it left the civilian air traffic control, the pilots' kicked it into another gear and they were soon traveling past the speed of sound.

Normally more than a six-hour flight, Hawley was now just an hour away from landing in Honolulu.

If ever there was a need for speed, this was it. Officially the Pearl Harbor briefing was called to discuss "a pressing issue of upmost concern," but Hawley knew the topic was the *Jiang Ding*, the Chinese Navy's new super-submarine. Nuclear-powered, nuclear-armed and touted by Beijing as an example of China's new global might, the futuristic U-boat had gone missing on its maiden voyage five days before.

The Chinese had been frantically looking for it ever since. While the sub's last known position was in the East China Sea about a hundred miles off Shanghai, the Chinese military established an enormous search grid, stretching from Shanghai almost down to the Taiwan Strait, and flooded the area with dozens of ships. But these waters soon became crowded as Russian, Japanese, and South Korean naval vessels also arrived, intent on looking for the sub on their own.

Within forty-eight hours it had become one of the largest, if surreptitious maritime searches ever. But at least for the moment, it was a massive fool's errand because the U.S. Navy had secretly found the sub the day before. Its environmental systems having failed, its 201-person crew suffocated, the *Jiang Ding* was now resting on the bottom, 210 feet down, about 80 miles north of where everyone else was looking for it.

Hawley would be ONI's sole representative at the Pearl Harbor briefing. The question to be put to him and the dozen other high-level attendees was simple: What should the U.S. do now that it had found the super-sub virtually intact, in international waters, at a depth not un-manageable for salvaging?

The national security implications were enormous—and Hawley was going to be right in the thick of it.

Looking out the window of the super-G, watching the sun set over the Pacific from 30,000 feet up, he could see his reflection in the double-thick pane of glass. Mid-60s, tall and bull-doggish-looking, he couldn't think of a bigger mission, with more importance or prestige, than the one that lay before him.

No matter what happened, he knew this case might be the crowning point of his career.

Or then again, maybe not . . .

They had just crossed the halfway point to Honolulu when Hawley saw the FASTEN SEATBELT light blink on. A moment later, the airplane went into a sharp bank and didn't stop until their direction had changed 180-de-grees.

Suddenly, the sunset was behind him.

Suddenly, he was heading back east.

One of the pilots came into the passenger compart-ment. He showed Hawley a decrypted message he'd just received on his secure cell phone.

The plane had been ordered to return to the United States and land at Hollywood-Burbank Airport where Hawley would receive new orders.

"Turn around?" he exclaimed on reading the text. "Why?"

The pilot just shrugged. "Something bigger has come up, I guess . . ."

Chapter Two

The G-60 landed ninety minutes later.

Night had fallen by now. But once away from the glare of the runway lights, Hawley could see the glow of Hollywood off to the south, about a 20-minute drive away.

He climbed out of the jet to find an all-black, tinted-windowed GMC waiting for him on the tarmac. Sitting in front was a Navy Commander named Jack Rooney and his Marine driver Sergeant Fisk. Both were in the early thirties, blonde and handsome. Both looked like movie stars.

Rooney directed Hawley into the back seat and then explained that they were from the Navy's Special Projects Support office.

"Never heard of you," Hawley told him.

"We expedite Navy personal and equipment for movies and TV, sir," Rooney explained. "Top Gun Two, NCIS Los Angeles and New Orleans. We also check scripts, make sure they're accurate and that the Navy is properly represented. If a production company needs a seaman's cap or an F-18, we're the office they go through."

Hawley took off his hat, unzipped his jacket and set-tled into the SUV's backseat. Several jobs came along with his position: one was senior operations officer for NILE, ONI's secretive law enforcement unit. They got missions either too sensitive or containing too many "un-anticipated elements" to give to the regular NCIS.

He was sure that's why he was here. But he couldn't imagine what NILE had to do with Rooney's Special Projects Support office.

"OK, proceed, commander," he said. "And it better be good."

Rooney tapped Sergeant Fisk on the shoulder. The marine punched an address into the vehicle's GPS, and off they went. Rooney turned back around to face Haw-ley again.

"Sir, I'm here to brief you on an incident that hap-pened earlier tonight during the taping of a TV reality show."

"A reality show?" Hawley stopped him. "I was turned around for an incident on a reality show?"

"The first-ever Pentagon-approved reality show," Rooney clarified. "We were told to find you and get you up to speed as soon as possible."

Hawley's head had already started to spin.

Where was this going?

"Start at the beginning, commander," he told Rooney. "And please, talk slowly."

The junior officer referred to notes on his mobile.

"The name of the TV program is 'America's Most Haunted—SEALs vs Hell House,'" he began. "It's on HBO. Five SEALs are supposed to spend the night in a haunted house—on TV. The goal is to 'capture the flag' at the top of the house, but they have to make their way through lots of special f/x and non-lethal weaponry— things like flash grenades, concussion grenades and smoke bombs, all supplied by Naval Special Weapons Command."

"Those idiots," the Admiral huffed. "Who the hell approved all this?"

Rooney looked embarrassed. He glanced at Sergeant Fisk, who just shrugged.

"Sixteen hundred, Penn, sir," Rooney said, lowering his voice. "Someone there sees it as a recruitment tool. A team from the 82nd Airborne is scheduled in for next week."

Hawley just rolled his eyes. "Continue, commander..."

"The show has a strange twist," he went on. "The house itself is almost impossible to get out of. The production company is able to literally lock the SEALs inside from dusk to dawn."

"How?" Hawley wanted to know.

"HBO bought ten million dollars' worth of titanium locks," Rooney told him. "They're wired to an unhackable micro-processing unit that makes them inoperable without the right pass codes. Then, HBO paid Lloyds of London another *fifty* million dollars to insure that each lock will work when called upon. Thirteen windows and two main doors, when they all close, the SEALs will be locked in there tight, alone, all night—or the Brits will eat the fifty million."

Hawley looked at his watch. He would have been landing in Honolulu right about now.

"Where the hell is all this taking place, Commander?" he barked at Rooney.

"In an old movie ranch up near San Fernando called Happy Valley," the man replied. "We are heading there right now. HBO is renovating the place. One set they call Spooky Street. That's where this Hell House is. Old Victorian mansion, up on a hill; fake graveyard out front. Lots of people recognize it from horror movies made in the 1950s."

The GMC was on the LA Freeway by this time and speeding north.

"This was the first TV production HBO was shooting at Happy Valley," Rooney went on. "But safe to say, it got off to a bad start . . ."

"And what exactly went wrong?" the Admiral finally asked him.

The navy officer started to say something, but stopped.

"Sir," he said instead. "You have to see for yourself."

The GMC arrived at the Happy Valley movie ranch just before 9 p.m.

The prop town was in a canyon deep inside the San Fernando Valley. Four different blocks with four different facades. Ghost movies, westerns, gangster films, war flicks, there was hardly a B-movie in the 1950s that wasn't shot out here.

Beyond the edge of the faux town, sitting atop a flat piece of high desert exactly one-half mile south of Hell House, was a collection of five enormous, pearl-white trucks. They were parked in a circle, a roaring campfire in the middle, looking like futuristic tour buses, each with a large satellite dish on top.

This was HBO Remote Control, an entire production studio on wheels. Just over a dozen people worked in the unit. Besides them and the residents of Hell House, there was no one else out here for miles.

Arriving at the encampment, Rooney led Hawley to the grandest production truck of all, Remote 1. Inside was a huge control room with a dozen TV consoles, a director's station and more than a hundred video monitors surrounding a larger 102-inch screen. All of it was dedicated to the America's Most Haunted show.

The place looked antiseptic and very high tech, but it smelled awful. Like a *vomitorium*; that's what popped into Hawley's head. Buckets of soapy water and bleach were in evidence. Mops, rags, air fresheners. Fans . . .

But nothing was helping. The smell was terrible.

The control room was empty except for one of the show's producers, a man named Owens. Of indeterminate age and dressed in a typical LA, sweater-tied-around-the-shoulders-way, Owens explained to Hawley what Rooney already knew: what he was about to see was video footage of what happened inside the Hell House earlier during the taping of the SEALs episode. He emphasized the raw TV feed had not been altered or edited in any way.

With Sergeant Fisk stationed outside the door, Owens led Hawley and Rooney to the main console where all three sat down.

The room darkened and the big TV screen above the console came to life.

***

A short time later, the side door of Remote 1 opened and Hawley staggered out.

He stumbled to a nearby trash can, stuck his head inside and vomited heavily, losing his cap and cell phone in the process.

The heaving went on for nearly a minute. When Hawley finally came up for air, he found Sergeant Fisk standing behind him with a bottled water in hand.

"Can I be of assistance, sir?" the marine asked him.

"I'm fine, son," Hawley replied with much embarrassment. But he took the water anyway.

"Permission to speak freely, sir?" Fisk asked.

Hawley took a few sips of water, just praying it would stay down.

"Only if it's brief," he croaked.

"Anyone who has seen that feed has had the exact same reaction as you," the marine driver told him. "When you see something so horrible happen right in front of you, it's enough to trigger severe digestive distress."

Hawley almost laughed. He was sure few admirals had ever found themselves in a less dignified position than this, blowing lunch into a trash barrel.

"Thank you, sergeant," he said, finally straightening up and breathing deeply. "I appreciate that information.

Now, if you could please lend me your cell phone? I need to make an important call."

Chapter Three

The two marines heard the car before they saw it.

A deep rumbling, the unmistakable racket of lots of horsepower coming their way.

Two headlights spearing the gloom, extra wide tires kicking up dust on the old desert road, a 1989 Jaguar XJS coupe appeared out of the morning mist. Five speeds, 12-cylinders, armored body and bullet-proof glass. The marine squad leader, a corporal, waved his flashlight, bringing the Jag to a halt next to an old rusty sign that read: "Welcome to Happy Valley."

The security checkpoint was a mile from the movie ranch itself and a half mile from the HBO Remote Control camp. This road was the only way in and out of the canyon.

The driver stopped, rolled down his window and handed his Navy service ID to the corporal.

"Lieutenant Chris Starr . . . here on orders from Admiral Hawley."

The corporal saluted and returned his ID.

They'd been expecting him.

Starr learned about the situation in Hell House in a most unusual way.

It was Friday night, game night for him and Angel. They were just about to commence when he heard his cell ringing in the other room. He let it go to voicemail as his mind was on other things at the time.

When the cell started beeping again five minutes later, he couldn't ignore it. What he found was a long recorded message left by the Admiral himself.

It went on for nearly five minutes, the longest communication he'd ever received from his pathologically aloof boss.

The next thing Starr knew, he was in the Jag, driving north, drinking coffee and not playing Superman anymore.

He'd shaved the normally two-and-a-half hour trip from San Diego to San Fernando down to an hour-ten, using two valuable weapons.

The Jag could top 150 MPH without breathing heavy. Plus, his short-term ESP sometimes let him know when the California Highway Patrol was about. More reliable than any police scanner, it was just a little voice, coming from who-knows-where, telling him: *Slow down.*

Whenever the voice spoke, he listened.

He'd replayed the Admiral's phone message a half dozen more times on his dash north. Even though it was relatively lengthy, the Admiral left some big holes in the story, telling Starr exactly what people had told him: You've got to see what happened for yourself.

As they should have, the two marines gave the Jag a thorough going over, including using infrared cameras to look under the chassis.

The corporal finally came back around to Starr's window. He had grime on his hands from reaching under the Jag's wheel wells.

"Excuse me, sir," the corporal began. "I never thought I'd be asking this question, but . . . do you have two machine guns installed in this car?"

"Yes, I do," Starr replied.

It was true. ONI had finally approved his request to arm the Jag, this after he'd detailed in quadruplet the number of armed encounters he'd had with adversaries in the past two years along with statistics and a graph proving extra firepower would have ended many of them quicker.

He had all the necessary clearances and paperwork in the glove compartment, but chose to make it simple. He flashed the corporal his ONI ID instead.

The marine got the message.

He saluted Starr again and sent him on his way.

A few minutes later, Starr was sitting inside the HBO Remote 1 production truck.

Owens was beside him, looking haggard and pale.

He started the raw tape at the beginning of the SEALs game, but then paused it.

"Do you mind if I step outside while this is playing?" he asked Starr. "I've seen it four times already and I just can't watch it again."

"No problem," Starr replied. The Admiral had made it clear that the video at the heart of the matter was extremely tough to watch.

So once Owens departed, Starr steeled himself, took a breath and then pushed the play button himself.

The video opened in the basement of the haunted house. A vast dark space, part of which had been turned into a sort of locker room, the five SEAL contestants were there, decked out in full special-ops regalia, including oversized Fritz helmets equipped with flip-down Night Vision goggles/video cams. Each was introduced in a three-second spot crammed with personal information, much like football players before a televised game. There was a lot of fist-pumping and syncopated high-fiving during these segments. It was like the SEALs were getting ready to play the Super Bowl.

A digital display in the lower part of the screen counted down the seconds to the beginning of the show feed. When the clock reached 00:00, the numbers turned red and started counting upwards. That's when all of the house's robot cameras and microphones came to life.

The production crew was shown putting their gear into one of the big white trucks and driving away. The last man out casually pushed a big red button that, as explained by graphics, started the video transmission beaming from the haunted house directly to the HBO Remote Control set-up on the ridge outside of town.

Then came a quick shot of the sun disappearing over the nearby mountains, followed by the twelve Lloyd's of London-insured locks dramatically slamming shut, one at a time, each with its own distinctive *bang!* The last to lock were the haunted house's front doors. They closed with an eerie creak quickly followed by two of the most thunderous bangs yet, bolting the SEALs inside.

A scroll at the bottom of the screen reviewed the rules of the game. The team had to make it to the attic of the haunted house by dawn and retrieve their unit flag in order to declare victory. But it would not be easy. The house was wired with dozens of the non-lethal weapons provided by the Navy itself. The worst of the lot were the non-lethal-weapon/improvised explosive devices—NLW/IEDs, or "newlyweds" in slang. The scroll revealed this particular team actually referred to the newlyweds as "FNFs" for reasons that HBO's censors would not let them reveal, hinting though it was sexual in nature.

Whatever their name, these booby-traps could be any combination of flash grenades, concussion grenades, pepper sprays or smoke bombs. But they were guaranteed to always be blinding bright and ear-busting loud.

If a team member tripped an FNF during the journey, he was declared killed in action and had to leave the house immediately. The only one way to do this: a device near the mansion's front doors would scan his retinas and then ask for a voice recognition code. Only then would the doors' superlocks open and allow him, and only him, to leave. Then the house would close up again and the survivors would continue the game.

The FNFs were not the only obstacles. A slew of horror-f/x generators had been planted throughout the house as well. Known as CGI packs, or Ciggies, these hidden projectors were able to produce holographic visions of warfare at its most ghastly—in full color and 3D. As many as a dozen of these sixty-second nightmares were scheduled to pop up randomly throughout the night to further hamper the SEALs.

Finally, the halls of the mansion were cluttered with horror-movie props, from rubber guillotines to paper mache electric chairs. Instruments of torture and death were hung on the walls, including cardboard axes and swords made of tin foil. Bogeymen like werewolves and vampires also haunted the corridors, their life size wax statues always placed in the darkest of their corners.

The SEALS would not be unarmed. Each would carry an M-4FX-65.2 laser rifle, designed especially by HBO for the show and known simply as M-4HBOs. Its laser shot could disable an FNF or a Ciggie, if the weapon was aimed correctly.

The TV feed went back to the SEALs and on a given signal they lowered their night vision goggles and gave a group thumbs-up to the cameras. All the lights in the house went out, sending the broadcast into the emerald world of NightVision as seen through the SEALs' helmet-cams.

On the first man's signal, the team aligned themselves in a standard, single-file house-clearing formation . . . and started to climb out of the basement.

The game had begun.

They made it up the basement's stairway and into the first-floor hallway, the drama of every step captured from a dozen angles. But they were not ten feet down the hall when the point man brushed against a wax figure of the grim reaper—and tripped an FNF.

It was a flash grenade connected to a concussion grenade—a Double Squealer. Tremendously loud and bright, even Starr jumped when it went off. There was so much light, the big screen was blotted out with static for five long seconds before returning to normal. Another few seconds passed before the SEALs got their sight and hearing back. Finally, they signaled to the cameras that all was OK.

Starr took a deep breath when it was over—only to nearly gag. The production truck smelled awful. He put his hand over his mouth and nose and returned to the show.

He watched as the guilty SEAL hung his head for nearly a half minute, before finally getting to his feet, bro-hugging his bros and making his exit, fading away in reality-show disgrace.

The game continued. once again creeping along the first-floor hallway, the four remaining players had their electronic eyes looking everywhere for FNFs or Ciggies. They safely reached the mansion's grand entryway, a large open space with a curving staircase going up one side. The SEALS needed to get to the second floor, and this was the only way up.

Now the new point man, the first-in-line SEAL, took one step onto the staircase—and all Hell broke loose. Suddenly the entryway was lit up with a storm of laser-generated tracer fire; hundreds of streaks of red fluorescent light were ricocheting everywhere, looking and sounding very much like the real thing. The SEALs squeezed themselves against the wall, but the tracers kept raining down on them, fired by unseen gunmen at the top of the stairs.

They were trapped.

A graphic explained this was where the game's "electronic paintballs" came into play. Contained within these laser bursts, were smaller, more condensed packets of energy nicknamed "toons." Like getting shot with a paintball, when a toon hit you, you knew it. A bee sting that turns into a burning sensation and then into a throbbing, dull pain, all in a few seconds—an unpleasant feeling, even for a fully armored SEAL. And if the Ciggie's computer determined you'd been hit with too many toons, then you too were declared KIA and would have to take the walk of shame out of the place.

But the SEALs did not falter. Firing their own laser weapons, and as seen through their own helmet-cams, the team went up the stairs double time, an absolute deluge of tracer streaks following their ascent, once again loudly blotting out the TV feed for a few moments.

Starr mistakenly took another deep breath, stunned by the realism of the CGI gun battle. In response, he felt his stomach both flip and tighten at the same time. He was sure it was the smell that was getting to him, whatever the hell it was. Taking off his ball cap, he used it to cover his nose and mouth and went back to the tape.

Battered by the barrage of electronic paint balls, the SEALs finally reached the second floor. But an even more unnerving vision awaited them. There was a long hallway to their left, at the end of which were the stairs to the third floor and above that, the attic and their prize.

But out of nowhere, the invisible Ciggie gunmen who had just been shooting at them were suddenly made very visible. Projected as especially fanatical terrorists, dozens of them came rushing down the hallway at the SEALs, firing their toon weapons and shouting intentionally obscure religious sayings at full volume.

The SEALs formed a defensive line across the hallway and fired back. Their fusillade was bright and noisy—and on target. Yet a good hit on any attacker only meant that he'd be replaced in a flash by another—and then another.

The battle became so intense, the CGI pyrotechnics blotted out the video feed for a third time. Starr squirmed in his seat, now even queasier. The last thing he'd eaten was a bowl of Wheaties, his ritualistic pregame night meal with Angel. But that had been more than four hours ago; and his stomach was just turning sour now?

By the time the TV feed had cleared, the video skirmish was over. The holographic attackers had vanished, and a disturbing quiet had come over the second-floor hallway.

Using hand signals, the SEALs silently formed up and began their march again.

Two seconds later, the front man tripped another FNF.

The game went into its second freeze as the guilty party was dispatched. Starr wished he'd snagged a bottled water or something before he started the show. His stomach was really starting to rumble.

Now down to three, and just halfway to their goal, the SEALs pressed on. But their boldness was only rewarded by a grand slam of Ciggie effects. The hallway suddenly turned into something from an Escher drawing. Up was both down *and* sideways. A moment later, the corridor seemed to stretch on forever. An instant after that, the stairway to the all-important third floor seemed unnaturally oversized, taunting the SEALs that the next part of their journey was tantalizingly in reach, but really not.

Then the ghosts showed up—and they were not Casper wannabees. As projected by the Ciggies, a dozen extremely real looking spirits suddenly appeared in the hallway. Men, women and, just to be extra creepy, children.

Some seemed oblivious to their surroundings, disturbing in itself. Others were staring at the SEALs and even trying to provoke them. Each time one spirit opened its mouth, it emitted a horrible cacophony of screams, provided in stereo by HBO. All this, as seen through the SEALs helmet-cams and the flash-cut editing of the Remote Control production team, was particularly unsettling, psycho-warfare at its best.

The SEALs tried firing at the ghosts, but it didn't work like that with the walking dead. Only hitting a Ciggie projector could stop the ethereal invasion, but the projectors were almost impossible to see in the low light.

So, the SEALs simply soldiered on. Trying their best to ignore the otherworldly holograms, they double-timed it down the hallway, running along the wall as if trying to escape a fire. In some cases, they were passing *right through* the spirits, always resulting in an extra-loud and chilling chorus of unearthly screams, especially from the child ghosts.

The madness finally ended when the SEALs reached the bottom of the third-floor stairway. But just as they started their ascent, the last man in line tripped yet another FNF, setting off a massive flash grenade and a cloud of smoke and pepper gas. The man was thrown backwards by the blast, setting off a second FNF, this one featuring a microwave-based laser weapon that gave its target the very real feeling they were being cooked from the inside out.

The other three SEALs were also affected by the twin blasts. The game went into a freeze once again until everyone recovered their sight and hearing.

Only then did the offender take his walk of shame.

Then there were two.

According to a graphic, they were CPO Butch Sterns on point, Master Chief Donn Kurjan about five feet behind, watching their six.

But Starr had to hit the pause button at that point; his stomach had grown even worse. As entertainment, the ghastly Ciggies alone were must-see TV. But nausea aside, why someone higher-up green-lighted the program was beyond him. It didn't show the SEALs in any heroic light. They'd already lost more than half their force to Hollywood generated horror and the Navy's own weapons—and all if it had been captured on video for millions to see.

Even if the two remaining men reached the attic and retrieved the flag, Starr didn't see this as being a good look for the SEALs or the Navy.

But at the same time, he wanted it to be over.

He pushed the play button and the tape resumed.

The remaining two SEALs climbed the third-floor stairs very carefully, CPO Sterns still in the lead. One step at a time, slowly putting one boot in front of the other, they were breathlessly reporting their progress to the outside world, like they were the first men to step on the Moon. With the video feed coming directly from their helmet-cams, their heavy breathing was being accentuated courtesy of HBO Remote Control. And everyone, including Starr, was just waiting for another frightening FNF to go off at any moment.

Yet somehow, the pair reached the top of stairs unscathed, a graphic reporting the heart rate and breathing in both men as being severely elevated and close to "critical levels." Still they paused for a moment of triumph, each giving a thumbs-up to the nearest camera.

Facing them now was a long, narrow, darkened hallway, its walls covered with bizarre artwork. At the far end was a fake hangman's gallows. A single upright post with a beam projecting from its top, it came complete with dangling noose and a chair to stand on and be kicked away at the moment of execution.

On the wall behind it, and illuminating it in a weird way, there was a large stained-glass window. Actually made of colored cellophane, it was one of several in Hell House. At its center was a bright pink rose, its pedals surrounding a medieval-style saddle.

Hanging from the ceiling above the gallows was a short white cord with a small plastic human skull on the end. A graphic explained this cord was attached to a pull-down ladder which led to the attic and the game's prize.

The two SEALs began moving forward again, the TV feed switching exclusively to Kurjan's night vision helmet-cam. He watched as the lead man Sterns approached the gallows cautiously, directing his flashlight up and down the contraption. He reported back to Kurjan that while he didn't want to touch the prop for fear it was booby-trapped, he had no choice as he would have to step up on its platform and then up on the chair under the noose in order to grab the annoyingly short white cord.

Kurjan concurred; it was their only move. Telling Sterns he would help by throwing more illumination on the gallows, he looked down at his utility belt to detach his own tac-light.

But in that brief moment, there was a flash of light so bright it blotted out the TV screen for nearly seven seconds, an eternity in TV time.

When the transmission came back online, Starr was shocked to see that the hangman's noose had somehow gotten around Sterns' neck and the chair had been kicked away. The SEAL was fighting it mightily, but the noose was not only choking him, it was inexplicably cutting through his skin, his muscles, his bones.

Helmet knocked off, his legs doing a disturbing spastic dance, Sterns clutched his bloody throat, let out one last horrific scream—and then his skull exploded.

Brain matter splattered everywhere. Pieces of cranium stuck to the ceiling and the walls. The amount of blood gushing out of the horrendous wound looked like it was coming from a fire hose at full pressure. Noose no longer holding it, the headless figure stood frozen for an instant before falling out of the frame.

A moment later, Kurjan either lost his footing or collapsed. He tumbled forward, smashing his helmet-cam to bits.

The TV feed went dead after that.

Chapter Four

Starr drove down to Happy Valley in fifth gear, hitting 70 mph along the bumpy road and leaving a great cloud of dust behind him.

It was just minutes before sunrise. He was steering with one hand and holding his Sig in the other. Full clip, one in the chamber, safety off. It didn't make any gunsense, but just like the twin 30s under the grille, it sure made him feel better. After what he'd just seen, he was ready to shoot anything that moved.

He roared onto Gangster Avenue, passing facades built to look so authentically like 1930s Chicago, they had real bullet holes in them. Turning left onto Cowboy Lane, he was suddenly speeding down a mud-caked main street of an old Western town. Signs for a saloon, a bank, a general store and a jail flashed by him.

Another sharp right and he was in bombed-out Berlin, circa 1945. Partially demolished buildings, burned-up tanks, skeletal jeeps and lots of fake barbed wire and prop debris. The place appeared old and sad at the moment, but he was sure it all looked real when it was on camera.

One more squealing right and he finally came to Spooky Street. There was a small, faux crypt on the corner; next door was a generic UFO crash site and then an artificial swamp for movie creatures to lurk beneath.

Then, on his right came the Hell House. Victorian-style, partially decayed mansion, two crooked trees guarding the entrance with a small graveyard out front. Starr had seen this place in dozens of horror movies and TV shows over the years. It looked familiar right away.

A blacked-out GMC was parked beside the corrugated tombstones, obviously, the Admiral's ride. Starr parked next it, holstered his Sig, and took a moment to breathe. The case was already making him sick; no wonder the control room smelled of puke.

He climbed out of the Jag and hurried up to the house. The Admiral was waiting on the front porch with two men Starr would learn were Commander Rooney and Sergeant Fisk. But that was it. As far as Starr could see, no one else was around.

He climbed the steps and saluted. Looking extremely disconcerted, Hawley barely saluted back. But as usual, he got right to the point.

"You saw the tape, lieutenant?" he asked.

"I did, sir . . ."

"And how's your stomach?"

"Oscillating, sir"

After quick introductions, Hawley led them through the front doors and into the house's grand entranceway.

Starr glanced around the hallway, trying to pick up any vibes. This place *was* a house, in that it had rooms and floors and ceilings. But like everything in Happy Valley, it was more facade than real. Everything appeared made of the cheapest plywood available, tacked onto odd cuts of planking that looked culled from a junk-yard.

Nothing was actually measured. Nothing was even close to exact. It was Hollywood; it didn't have to be real. It just had to look that way.

"Are the remains still on site, sir?" Starr asked Hawley gravely.

The Admiral slowly shook his head no.

"That's another development," he said keeping his voice low. "The remains are . . . unaccounted for at the moment."

That was not what Starr was expecting.

No remains?

He also lowered his voice; microphones were everywhere.

"Judging from the way the deceased met his end," he half-whispered to Hawley, "it would seem that a substantial amount of at least partial remains would have been, well . . . evident around the scene."

"I'm well aware of that, lieutenant," Hawley replied wearily. "But the HBO production guys went through this place a dozen of times trying to find something—anything—but with no luck. I've been up to the third floor myself. Lots of dried blood, but no body. No body parts. Nothing."

Starr didn't need ESP to know something was gigantically wrong here—but for a moment, he wondered if the solution might be right in front of them.

"Special effects?" he asked the Admiral. "Something maybe malfunctioned in that remote video room—accidentally on purpose?"

But Hawley was emphatically shaking his head no.

"The HBO guys swear this is not some kind of publicity stunt," he replied. "They shut down everything the second it happened and that had to cost them a bundle of money. Besides, they seem just as freaked out about all this as we are. You must have met Owens. He's having kittens over this whole thing—and his bosses are screaming at him for some kind of explanation."

"What about the other SEAL, then?" Starr asked Hawley quietly. "Master Chief Kurjan . . . the number two man? The guy who saw it all? Where is he?"

"Long gone before I got here," Hawley said. "The HBO guys put out a call for the nearest EMTs and he was rushed to San Fernando Mercy Hospital, about thirty miles from here. They thought they were doing the right thing, I guess. Apparently Chief Kurjan was really flipping out."

"But they compromised our only witness," Starr said, trying his best to face away from the mics.

"The whole place has been compromised, lieutenant," Hawley told him. "Like I said, after the SEAL disappeared, HBO shut down the feed and twelve of them rushed over here. By the time they finally got inside, there was no sign of CPO Sterns, except all that blood."

"But how did they get in, sir? I thought that was impossible once the sun went down?"

Hawley motioned for Commander Rooney to join the conversation. He re-asked Starr's question.

"The HBO contract states that in the event of serious injury or worse, production has to cease immediately," Rooney explained, also in hushed tones. "Of course, they never expected anything like this to happen. But once it did, the HBO crew tried to get into the house through the one and only emergency access door. It's in the rear of the building; it's a crawl space and is never mentioned on the broadcast. They added it only to satisfy the local fire warden.

"Now . . . it too was held by a Lloyd's of London lock, part of the deal, but separate from the rest of the grid and to be opened only in an absolute crisis. But when the crap hit the fan, the code originally given to them by Lloyds didn't work. This led to a flurry of calls to London to get a delete code and then a new code to enter. In the meantime, Lloyd's attorneys called HBO's attorneys and insisted they sign a waiver, removing this lock from the list of insured locks. All this took more than an hour before the emergency door finally got opened. The dozen HBO techs went in and rushed to the third floor. But, like the Admiral said, they found nothing there but the dried blood."

"Those guys had turned this place inside out twice before I even got the call," Hawley told Starr. "Some of them even tried recreating what happened—but with no joy. Like it or not, HBO is up to their shorts in this thing now. Lucky for us, they're team players. Unlucky for us—well, you know . . ."

Starr knew. Good intentions aside, the HBO production people were not trained in search operations or criminal investigations. With twelve of them tramping all over the house, leaving fingerprints, footprints, bits of saliva and DNA everywhere, they might have destroyed the very evidence needed to solve the case on the spot.

"This is really going to be starting at ground zero," Starr sighed.

Hawley and Rooney exchanged worried looks.

"Well . . . we have another issue here, lieutenant," the Admiral said. "Something else we have to address. Something we can file under 'unanticipated elements.'"

That was code inside NILE for something totally fucked-up. Dealing with unanticipated elements was why people inside ONI called NILE the X-Files Guys.

"More 'unanticipated' than what I just saw on the tape?" Starr asked him. "Or the fact that the remains haven't been found?"

Hawley gave Rooney a quick nod.

"I can't believe I'm saying this," the junior officer began. "But while the HBO people were searching for CPO Sterns, they could hear him . . ."

"Hear him, sir?"

"When they were searching for him," Rooney tried to explain. "They started hearing a man's voice. Coming from inside the walls. Calling out for help."

"I thought they were nuts," Hawley interjected. "But they'd recorded it and they played it for me. And goddamn, I heard him, too. We all did . . ."

The Admiral's voice almost cracked on saying this. Rooney and Sergeant Fisk agreed.

"It was another very unpleasant experience," Rooney said glumly.

"Total creep show," Fisk added.

"I'd arrived by that time," Hawley went on. "Soon after I saw that tape, I texted Maryland and they ordered me to contain whatever the hell was going on out here. That meant everyone who'd been inside the house had to be brought to a secure location and kept there indefinitely. Twelve of them. They're at a National Guard barracks just outside the valley."

"It had to be done," Starr agreed. "But again, just to be sure, sir, is there any reason we shouldn't believe everything HBO is telling us about their special effects? I mean, missing bodies, voices in the walls? It sounds like something is malfunctioning . . ."

But once more, Hawley emphatically shook his head no. "I asked that guy Owens point-blank if this was some nutty way to promote his show. I reminded him that every SEAL I know can be nasty in his own way, especially the retired ones. When they lose one of their own, they become upset."

"And how did he respond?"

"In the most rational voice possible," Hawley answered. "He asked me: 'Do you really think we'd screw with the SEALs?'"

Starr turned to Rooney. "When was this show supposed to air, sir?"

"This Sunday night, right after the four o'clock NFL games," he replied. "It's a pay for view event and HBO has promoted the hell out of it. They've also taken in a lot of money for it already. So on Sunday night, millions of people are going to be expecting *something* having to do with SEALs inside Hell House. That means HBO *has* to put out a program, or the whole ship might go down."

It was obvious Hawley was hearing this for the first time. He did not like it.

"Commander, a man is missing here and maybe dead," he said. "Are we really talking about TV ratings?"

But Rooney stood his ground.

"The problem isn't ratings, sir," he said, politely but firmly. "It's perception. We all know who at the top approved this thing, but it's got 'U.S. Navy' written all over it. And if we can't figure this out by tomorrow at the latest, it will move beyond our control. We're already holding twelve HBO people. Their families are going to want to know where they are. People will start getting dribs and drabs of news, stir it altogether and then, at the very least, accuse us of a cover-up."

The Admiral didn't like hearing this either, but he was coming around to Rooney's way of thinking.

"OK, commander," he said. "So, how do we avoid getting locked in that box?"

Rooney just shrugged.

"Find the guy," he said.

Chapter Five

That's what they tried to do . . . for the next nine hours.

Starr and Hawley started at the top of the mansion with plans to work their way down. After strict orders from Hawley not to touch anything they found of interest, Rooney and Fisk started in the basement and would work their way up.

All the Ciggies and FNFs were turned off, by design they couldn't operate in daylight anyway. HBO had killed all the cameras and mics as well. For the purposes of investigation and in an effort to solve the case quickly before word leaked out, it was just the four Navy members in the house. Those few employees still at the HBO Remote camp a half mile away stayed there with orders not to use any communications devices.

For nine hours, Starr and Hawley looked here, there and everywhere for any sign of CPO Sterns. The Admiral, his top boss, a guy who, in the past, had barely spoken to him, was now helping him look for a missing body inside a haunted house.

Sometimes, things just happen.

Their first stop had been the infamous attic with its pull-down ladder. But on arrival, the place turned out to be just that . . . an attic. A bunch of old props stored away and forgotten, a few long-ago burned-out Klieg lights and that was it. The rest was just dust.

Sitting amongst the junk, held in a faux-bronzed trophy cup, was the SEAL team's unit flag. Starr saw finding it as a bittersweet moment; Hawley did not.

"All this, for this?" he grumbled, pushing the trophy aside.

Just before the video caught CPO Sterns in his death dance, there had been a flash of light so bright, it knocked everyone's NVGs off-line for almost seven seconds. Though it was hard to tell, the light might have come from the attic.

But there was nothing up here that could have emitted such a flash. No antique projectors, no battery of old show lights. There weren't even any electrical outlets to plug into.

They checked the attic's fake walls, floors and ceiling, but found no warm spots, no indications that anything odd had happened up here at all.

They finished scanning the room then paused a moment to take it all in. Hawley looked and moved like someone completely out of place. They were both still queasy.

"Thoughts, lieutenant?" he finally asked.

"Full disclosure sir?'

"Of course . . ."

Starr took another look around the room. "I have to say a lot of things here are indicating some kind of bizarre special effects," he said.

Hawley just shrugged. "That's now in the back of my mind too, lieutenant, more so with every minute. But would HBO be prepared to jump through all these hoops and many more to come—just for a publicity stunt?"

Starr shrugged back. "Big audience gets a lot bigger if something like this gets leaked before tomorrow night."

"And make the Navy look like the chumps?" Hawley asked worriedly.

"It *is* TV, sir," Starr told him. "Ever watch the Army-Navy game? The TV coverage is always brutal to the Navy side. Cameras, direction, cheering squads. Consistently terrible . . ."

Hawley nodded wearily. "I've noticed that," he said. "But would HBO really want to make enemies of the U.S. Navy? If that was the case, they could forget about doing anything with the Pentagon ever again. This whole Hell House concept involves all of the service branches. They'd be killing their own golden goose."

The senior officer glanced around the dusty room again, the bare sunlight making its way through the yellow-gelled plastic window panes.

"No, I still trust them," he concluded. "They're Hollywood guys, but I can't believe they'd pull a prank like this."

He paused a moment and then added: "I just think something else is going on here."

They climbed down the drop ladder and examined the gallows itself. Again, it wasn't a real, functioning execution machine. It was fake, though it had played a big part in the unseemly departure of CPO Sterns.

The gallows' platform was about two feet off the floor. It was stained with dried blood, as was the old, tattered carpet surrounding it. Yet despite the splatter, there had been no sign of Sterns' body—or his body parts—when the HBO crew finally reached the scene of the incident. This only led to another mystery.

"How could something so extraordinarily bloody as Sterns' corpse suddenly disappear in a house that no one can enter or leave?" Hawley said now, running his hand along the rickety gallows.

Starr grimaced, wet his finger, took a sample of the dried blood and put it to his tongue.

"This might not be his blood," he said starkly. "It might be pig's blood."

Hawley looked at him crosswise. "How do you know?" he asked, totally mystified.

But Starr just shook his head, almost embarrassed.

"I don't know, sir," he said quietly. "I just do . . ."

Down and up and up and down, they went; meeting Rooney and Fisk so many times in the middle it became the running joke.

There was no break, no water, no coffee. They scoured every inch of the house, even removing pieces of the fake walls in some places, only to find the back of another fake wall facing them.

Under the floorboards, up through the ceilings. They even checked the chimney.

Nothing.

When it got near to 7 p.m. with a 7:45 sunset on tap, they reconvened back in the grand entranceway. It had been a completely fruitless day. They were no closer to figuring out what happened here.

"Plan B?" the Admiral asked Starr dryly. "Before we tear the place down, plank by plank."

Starr could only shake his head. He could use some help here, but so far, his STPA2 had remained dormant.

A buzzing mobile phone disturbed the silence. Sergeant Fisk answered it, had a brief conversation, and then handed the phone to Rooney. Walking a few steps away, the officer had an even shorter conversation and then returned looking especially gaunt.

"We've just got another problem handed to us," he reported. "We just found out that two days before this even happened, the HBO public relations people had already floated a story to TMZ that something weird happened at Hell House—all while denying whatever happened was part of the show. Someone at TMZ connected to one of the twelve HBO employees we're holding called the police looking for their friend and referencing the story. Now the LA cops want to get involved."

Hawley doubled over, his hands going right to his knees, like an athlete trying to catch his breath.

He laughed tiredly. "I don't even want to think what comes next," he said. "The LA cops? Really?"

"They never met a camera they didn't like," Fisk said.

Hawley turned back to Starr.

"Well, this is why you're here, lieutenant," he said. "Do you have any magic dust you can throw around in time to get us out of this?"

Starr wished it was that easy.

A highly trained SEAL meets a ghastly end—but then vanishes basically on live TV, leaving very little behind. There was only one real connecting point. Whatever happened, happened at night, when the haunted house was sealed up tight.

If they couldn't find the answer in the daylight hours, then reason dictated that someone had to look for it at night—and under circumstances closest to when the gruesome incident took place.

"I'll stay in here tonight," Starr suddenly declared. "Get locked in, turn everything back on, see what happens."

The three others were shocked.

Hawley was the first to speak.

"I don't see the wisdom in that, lieutenant," he said. "At the very least I can get those two marines watching the entrance to be in here with you. Or the four of us will stay . . ."

But Starr was shaking his head no.

"I can't believe I'm saying this, sir," he told Hawley. "But I think in this case I have to work alone."

Chapter Six

Admiral Hawley promised Starr that if anything went wrong, the first line of his after-action report on Hell House would read: "Lieutenant Christopher Starr meritoriously volunteered to enter the activated facility alone in an attempt to bring about a quick solution of the matter."

It was odd to prepare for such a report so far ahead of time, but this was a very odd situation.

They were all suddenly living in this weird little world, away from everything else. Hawley, Rooney, and especially HBO, needed to be ready for anything.

It took a while for Starr to convince the Admiral that for his STPA2 to work, he had to experience the same conditions the SEALs did before Sterns vanished. That meant being inside the haunted house with all the Ciggies, FNFs, cams and mics turned on and all doors and windows sealed by their multimillion-dollar padlocks. Should he need any assistance while inside, he could signal the cameras and help could gain entry via the no-longer insured, emergency hatch in the back.

It was nuts, but in the end, Hawley just let him go. Too tired, too baffled by what was going on, Honolulu seemed like a long-lost dream to him now. Dealing with

NILE was always a pain in the ass because they were always involved in such murky stuff. But it was for situations exactly like this that Starr was plucked out of Naval Aviation and dropped into the lap of ONI.

Hawley just decided to let him earn his pay.

The sun went down and all the doors and windows in Hell House slammed shut with a cannon-shot series of electronically enhanced thuds.

The two front doors were the last to go. Once they were closed, titanium bolts six inches thick appeared from the ceiling and the floor and locked into place, just like in a prison movie.

Starr had positioned himself close by, wanting to witness the dramatic lock-up up close. He had nine hours and forty-eight minutes to cover the fake mansion, but the entryway was the heart of the place. This is where he wanted to take the audial blow—and it proved as dramatic as he'd imagined.

He was wearing a complete SEAL battle outfit, armored head to toe, an oversized Fritz helmet with built-in NVGs on top. He was also carrying one of the M-4HBO laser rifles. If the ciggies were as realistic as they seemed on video, he wanted something he could at least fight back with.

And in case things got really weird, when no one was looking, he'd dropped his Sig into his boot holster.

Seven still in the clip, one still in the chamber.

Once the house was sealed up, it became completely dark inside. Like a coffin after they close the lid.

Starr stayed in place, waiting. Only gradually did the recessed lighting along the high ceilings come to life. The low-power LCD bulbs provided just enough illumination for night vision feeds to show up on video and that was it. But the gloomy shadows they cast only made the place even spookier.

Starr powered up his NVGs, immersing himself in their familiar emerald glow. He took a moment to focus on the mission. He was here, in a fake haunted house, trying at the very least to solve the disappearance of SEAL Chief Petty Officer Butch Sterns, whose remains were unaccounted for, yet, whose voice had been reportedly heard coming from behind the walls.

It was a mouthful, yes. And while he liked ONI to think he usually worked alone, sometimes Starr needed extra help with his crime-solving. He knew right away this was one of those times.

With everything up and operating inside the house, he moved down the hallway to a spot he'd scouted out before taking this plunge of faith. It was in a small, recessed space made to look like a cloakroom. Hawley, Rooney, Fisk and Owens—and only them—were back at HBO Remote watching the multi-camera transmission. But Starr was certain they couldn't see him in this cubby hole, and that the multitude of microphones could not hear him either.

He stepped inside, took out his rebuilt Tomato Can and hurriedly punched in a 22-number code. Hearing two beeps, he entered another, ten-digit number.

The phone rang once, and then: "Hello? Chris? Are you all right?"

It was Angel.

She and he were not supposed to have access to the slightly outdated U.S. Navy satellite phone, but, truth was, they used it to talk to each other all the time.

"All's OK, honey," he told her, hand over his mouth, not wanting to stay out of sight too long. "But I have to make this quick. Are you sitting down?"

"Why? How crazy is it?"

"Super-crazy," he replied.

He gave her the thumbnail: HBO, the show, Rooney's Hollywood unit, the Admiral, the SEAL's grisly disappearance. He was committing at least three Security Act violations in doing so, but sometimes, this was how he got things done.

"There's something really off about this place," he told her. "I know it's outfitted as a 'haunted house,' but I mean the structure itself has a weird buzz to it."

He could already hear her banging away on her laptop, calling up information on Happy Trails and Hell House.

"I'm on it," she told him.

Before going into the haunted house Starr had asked Owens for a copy of the raw tape of the incident; the HBO producer gave him the entire thing on a thumb drive. Starr now put that thumb drive into the side of the Tomato Can and sent the footage to Angel.

"Don't feel like you have to watch it all," he warned her. "Once they reach the top of the third-floor stairs, it gets pretty graphic."

"I'll block my eyes," she kidded him. "Now go, quick. Keep me in the loop and please be careful . . ."

"Your wish is my command," he replied.

His Tomato Can beeped twice and she was gone.

He took the next few minutes surveilling the entranceway, especially the inside of the two sealed front doors.

All the bolting mechanisms and power supplies seemed in order, as was the retina ID-processing station used by those contestants getting the boot. He studied a few first-floor window locks too, curious how secure the million-dollar slide bolts really were. But like the front doors, from all that he could see, Superman himself might have a hard time breaking out of here.

He finally headed to the basement. The plan from here was to retrace the steps of the SEAL team, reenacting their climb to the third floor as closely as he could. This was not any kind of scientific approach to investigating, though; he was just hoping his pre-cog would kick in soon and give him an assist.

He found the basement just as before—one big dark empty room that had been turned into a temporary staging area for the SEAL contestants. Lots of discarded paperwork; some used MRE containers on the floor. But he didn't see anything out of place. He started back towards the stairway out. But then . . . he stopped.

After thinking a moment, he reached down and pushed the M-4HBO's power button to On.

That was a mistake.

The moment the f/x rifle's power light blinked green, the basement suddenly erupted in laser gunfire.

It was coming right at him from the darkest recesses of the room. He took multiple laser hits to his upper body, instantly appreciating just how painful it was to be hit by a toon bullet—multiplied by six.

He fell to the floor and started firing back at the shadows. Because the Ciggie barrage was programmed to recreate a real gunfight, his return fire temporarily silenced the incoming. This led him to a lightning-quick, two-part plan: he would spray the interior of the basement and hope for another calm in the storm of laser tracers pinging all around him. Then he'd make a run for the stairs.

This would have been the perfect time for his STPA2 to kick in. Being a few seconds ahead of a bullet usually gave you enough time to duck—and most times that's all you needed. But his pre-cog was still not firing, so he'd have to run the gauntlet unassisted, like a normal human being.

He took a deep breath and squeezed his trigger. The whole room lit up as once again his outgoing laser tracers momentarily overpowered the Ciggie barrage. But in that micro-second before he launched himself towards the door, he could see hidden in the room's shadows, briefly illuminated by the ultra-realistic f/x, at least a dozen ghostly blackened faces, his CGI assailants, glaring back at him. It was shocking how real they looked.

In the next breath, he was gone, zig-zagging across the room, through the door and up the narrow staircase.

The firing stopped as soon as he reached the top step, but he did not survive unscathed. He'd been hit by another dozen laser bullets up across his back. Now he felt like he'd been stung by a hundred bees, the pain was intense and throbbing.

He paused to catch his breath. Brief as it was, that had been authentically horrifying. Had he been a contestant on the show, he'd been gone at this point—but he didn't even have that option. While all the house's gizmos were turned on, the game was not. This meant in theory the brutal f/x could shoot him up without mercy and even a cyber death could not spare him.

He took another moment to get himself together and return to the task at hand. He was back up on the first floor. The grand hallway and its staircase were just ahead of him. Next task: get to the second floor.

Readjusting his NVGs, he raised the laser rifle up in front of him and slowly started down the hallway.

On the third step he tripped a pair of FNFs.

The one, two flash of ultra-bright lights almost knocked him on his butt. Then came the noise—not ear-splitting, more like brain-splitting, a searing hot knife going in one side and out the other. He clutched his chest and went down on one knee.

He couldn't hear and he couldn't see—for nearly a minute. But Starr remained frozen longer than that. Still on one knee, he counted down five minutes, one second at a time, before he dared move a muscle.

Only then did he slowly readjust into a sitting position, his back against the wall, still at the bottom of the steps, with every movement, praying he would not set off another booby-trap.

Though his plan for the moment was to stay still and stay chill, in reality, he was a mess inside. He'd learned how real and traumatic the mind-bending pseudo-combat inside Hell House could be. But he also knew what might be coming next could be even worse.

Sitting there in the dark, a familiar anxiety began to bubble up inside him, not unexpected, but only adding fuel to his still-gyrating stomach. Old empty buildings sometimes presented a bad situation for him for a strange reason: he often heard dead people talking inside them.

It was an unfortunate offshoot of his STPA2, and it was nowhere as cool as the movie. Growing up—any old church, or funeral home, or hospital—he heard voices. Lots of them. Overlapping conversations going on all around him. Men, women, children. Never laughing, frequently crying. The voices of *real* ghosts, sounding morose and unearthly.

Even as a kid, he knew this was not normal—but he never said anything to anybody until the Navy shrinks told him he'd been right all along, he *wasn't* normal.

Just why he could tune in to some kind of afterlife radio, the Navy hadn't figured that out yet. An extremely uncomfortable feeling, there were some downsides to his pre-cog shrinkage. This was one of them.

It went on for what seemed like hours.

Hunched up against the wall, NVGs turned off, the voices were suddenly everywhere. Bouncing off the walls around him. Shaking the cheap-plank floor beneath him. He even imagined he could feel paint chips falling from the old ceiling, shaken loose by the ghostly vibrations.

But . . . then something changed.

It was barely perceptible at first. But as the seconds passed by, it became clear that at least some of the voices were moving towards him.

He held on, trying very hard to keep his stuff together. This was something he'd never experienced before. The voices of the dead always surrounded him, random, coming from everywhere and nowhere at the same time. This time it seemed like a group of them were right in front of him.

He slowly reached up and snapped his NVGs back on.

There was a blast of green static—and suddenly he realized just inches from his face . . . was another face. It was bloody, its mouth was drooling, half its forehead was missing, and its brain was pulsating. With everything but the stink, a decaying zombie was almost nose to nose with him. And behind this one, at least a dozen more, even more horrible-looking.

Starr hit himself upside the head, hurting his hand on the lip of the over-size Fritz helmet. He thought he could hide from the Ciggie projectors.

But he was wrong.

He just started firing. Back and forth, the M-4HBO on full auto, the light blinding him via the NVGs. It lasted for exactly a minute, and only then did the Ciggie's control system hit the stop button, and everything was supposed to go back to dark and be quiet again.

But even when all the CGI commotion died down, way in the background, Starr heard something that was still . . . out of place.

The hallway went nearly pitch black. But it didn't go quiet.

A man's voice.

Somewhere in the walls.

Crying out for help. Or maybe just crying.

Starr did not move—but the voice slowly faded away. He stayed still for a full minute and just listened. But it did no good.

The voice was gone.

He walked the first floor of the haunted house for the next two hours, hoping to hear the voice again.

In and out of the fake bedrooms, all of them shaped like oblongs, all of them with creaky floors and used mostly for storage. He twice circled around the so-called ballroom which was just an extra big oblong room behind the grand entranceway.

But, despite it all, he failed to pick up the voice again.

Sometime around midnight, he climbed the staircase to the second floor unopposed and began the same process. In and out of all the rooms, looking and listening, trying to be as thorough as possible. At the very least, he hoped he was putting on a good show for those watching back at HBO Remote Control. But in reality, his STPA2 was still not flashing on anything good. Even worse, after battling his own demons and hearing the ghostly voices, the place was *really* starting to give him the creeps.

It got to the point where he caught himself thinking the unthinkable: sending a signal to the cameras to get him out of the house and then reevaluate where to go from there.

In other words, give up.

Not like him.

But then, just as he was passing by the stairway that led up to the third floor, he heard the voice again.

It was coming from under the stairwell.

A man crying . . .

And this time he was certain it was real.

According to the Admiral, when the HBO search party first heard the voice, they'd tried talking back to it, but only got more sobbing. All attempts at making contact had failed.

But now, Starr couldn't resist.

He crouched down next to the stairwell, took off his helmet and put his ear to the wallboard.

There it was.

That whimpering . . .

Somewhere close, but also sounding very far away.

Starr didn't call out to it. Instead, he started knocking on the wall.

And after the third try, someone knocked back.

Chapter Seven

Starr spent the next two hours rapping on the stair-well wall, on all the walls around it, and those up and down the second-floor hallway, trying his best to communicate with the other side.

But no one knocked back. Just that one time, three slow raps in response to his and that was it. He wound up where it had started, next to the steps leading up to the third floor, the place he'd purposely saved searching for last.

Or least, that's what he told himself. Truth was, he'd been hoping he'd come upon something on the second floor or below that might solve the case, so it wouldn't have to go up to the third story at all.

But by four a.m., he couldn't avoid it any longer.

He took a deep breath and put his foot on the first step. At almost the same moment, the voices of the dead started drifting back to him.

He stopped on that bottom step, shut his eyes again and tried to fight them off. But it was like trying to fight off a bad dream—and it did no good. The whispers grew into a familiar symphony of the bleak and frightening and soon they were all around him.

Nothing in his experience could ever match the uncomfortableness of that moment or the fear that someday, it might last forever.

But then suddenly, his Tomato Can rang . . . and he was saved.

It was Angel.

"Hello, honey," he said, more grateful than she would ever know. "I feel bad that you're up so late."

"You won't feel that way when I tell you what I have to tell you," she replied in typical Angel-speak.

But with those words and just her voice, all the creepiness disappeared. The cries, the wailing, all gone. That was Angel's superpower: chasing the bad stuff away.

Plus, she was really good at playing detective.

"Tell me everything," he said, casually walking back down to the first floor and slipping into his hideaway cubby hole.

"Those HBO guys hyped that place as being in every ghost film from the Fifties, right?" she began. "But it has a much longer history than that. They were shooting films there way back in the 1920s. It was used in the first real B-movies, horror films, but also westerns and ordinary murder mysteries, most of them silent. Back in those days, the interior of the house could be made to look like just about anything. Saloon, haunted house, infirmary. Mad scientist lab."

"The magic of the movies," he said.

"Exactly. But that place already had built-in hidden panels, trapdoors and other crazy stuff used in those early movies. It came back to life in the Fifties and early Sixties, but then that whole B-movie thing kind of went away for good. It closed down again until HBO came across it for their TV shows."

Starr was amazed by the new information.

"Where did you get all this?" he asked her.

"Wikipedia," she laughed. "So you know it has to be true. But there's more . . ."

"Please tell me . . ."

"Well, do you think HBO knew ahead of time they were taping that show in a *real* haunted house?"

Starr laughed under his breath. "I'm not sure there is such a thing . . ."

"Want to bet?"

He didn't. She always won.

"Please, just tell me . . ."

"Back in the late Sixties, a few years after Hollywood abandoned the place a second time, that house was occupied by some, let's say, very unusual squatters. But the head of this little troop quickly came to believe the place was haunted because it had been built on an ancient Native American burial ground. He saw the ghosts; he talked to the dead—and he stayed there, in that house, for exactly one night, and even that was too much for him. He and his family cleared out the next day."

"His family?"

"The *Manson* Family, Chris," she said finally. "That place freaked out even Charlie Manson."

Starr nearly dropped the Tomato Can.

"Angel, honey," he replied. "You do realize that I'm alone in this place, right?"

"But I'm here with you," she said so sweetly he wanted to go right through the telephone to her. "Besides, I found something else, research-wise . . ."

"Please just tell me . . ." he said again, now almost comically.

"I'm watching a movie on the Cowboy Channel at the moment called 'The Haunted Saddle.' It was filmed there, in that house, in 1927. It's a silent-movie horror western—I didn't think there was such a thing. But it's about a ranch hand who disappears in that house."

"No way . . ."

"Way," she said. "And from the looks of the movie, that place hasn't changed at all since they filmed it. I'm about halfway through it right now and I can tell you that architecturally it's the same inside. When you compare it to the raw feed you sent me, it's obvious the renovations HBO did were not structural. I think they just put in a bunch of cameras and wired the place for sound.

They might not even know all those old f/x are still in there."

It was at that moment, like a bolt of lightning, the good part of Starr's STPA2 finally kicked in. It came in a flash, literally an electrical flash, before his eyes.

Go where he went . . .

That's all it said. That's all he needed. Angel knew what was happening. Starr was rarely quiet for very long in these situations—unless he was getting messages from the beyond.

"Are you in a storm?" she asked, their code for this sort of thing.

"I am," he replied, now abuzz with STPA2.

He was suddenly running up the stairway, down the second-floor hall and up to the third floor. He set off a trio of FNFs in the process, but was by them so quickly, they had little effect. He also triggered a Ciggie halfway up the stairs which created an army of zombies in combat uniforms waiting for him at the top. But again, he didn't care. They weren't real. He used the M-4HBO like a scythe, sweeping them out of his way.

Once on the third floor, he studied the narrow corridor beyond. At the end of it, in the low-light murk, were the fake gallows and the infamous drop-ladder, left in the down position.

And everywhere, dried blood that Starr had cosmically determined did not belong to CPO Sterns.

He climbed onto the gallows and went up the drop ladder. One step at a time, his first visit to the attic after dark.

It looked different via night vision. Green flares of a light were zipping all around the small space even though there were no electrical sources up here.

He stopped for a moment at the top of the ladder and then carefully put his foot down onto the attic floor.

Nothing . . .

He took another step, pressing down as hard as he could on the creaky floorboard.

Still nothing.

"Angel, are you still there?"

"With every step," she replied in a hushed voice. "And I apologize for what I said earlier. I wish you weren't alone there. And suddenly I wish I wasn't alone here either . . ."

He walked around the attic slowly. But his body just wasn't buzzing with the same intensity.

Then he realized something: No SEAL ever made it to the attic.

So what was he doing up here?

He went back down the ladder and now turned his attention to the fake gallows. It was just a thick post with a beam running out from the top and a noose hanging from it. It hadn't looked functional the first time he'd examined it and it certainly didn't now.

But, dead or alive, this is where SEAL Chief Butch Sterns was last seen.

He examined the gallows platform directly beneath the noose; this was where the biggest splat of dried blood was located. He and the Admiral had examined its wooden planks several times during their search earlier. But now, in the dark, with his NVGs on, Starr could see the floorboards were actually cut in an irregular pattern, and that, incredibly, the dried blood seemed to have filled in the oddly running cracks, almost as if to camouflage them.

He ran his fingers along these zig-zag configurations until he reached the edges of a perfect square. That's when he knew the gallows platform was actually a Mac-Gregor floor, used by early movie stunt men and illusionists all over.

He took the butt of his M-4HBO and slammed it against the center of the floorboards. They parted, just as they were designed to . . . and down he went.

It was not a straight shaft. It was a corkscrew-type slide, made with highly polished metal like something in an old-fashioned playground.

He did three 360-degree circuits before hitting the pitch-black bottom and landing in a heap, knocking out his NVGs.

When he turned them back on, the first thing he saw were . . . skeletons.

They were covering the floor all around him, none of them intact. But just by a quick bone count, he knew he was looking at least six bodies—or that's how it seemed. Because when he actually touched one of them, he realized they were made out of cardboard—fake, like everything else in the haunted house.

But then he looked up and saw something ten feet away from him that was very real. Crumpled in the far corner was the missing SEAL, CPO Butch Sterns—head still attached, dried tear stains on the cheeks.

Starr crawled over to him and put his hand on his neck.

Incredibly, he felt a pulse.

"You've got to be kidding me," he said out loud.

The SEAL was hurt, but still alive.

And maybe a little delusional.

Starr gently slapped him awake. When Sterns came to, his eyes went wide, and he immediately tried to speak. Starr told him not to. While he had a million questions for him, right now job one was to get Sterns out of the pit. His debriefing would come soon enough. Plus, who knew if there were any microphones down here?

When Sterns tried to talk a second time, Starr ordered him to be quiet.

But the SEAL insisted.

"Are you from HBO?" he finally croaked to Starr. "Because I've got to renegotiate my contract . . ."

Chapter Eight

It took Starr twenty minutes to climb back up the slippery, corkscrew slide—a very awkward ascent.

He crawled out of the MacGregor door and let it spring back into place, once more disguising itself as the gallows platform. He signaled thumbs-up to the cameras, relieved they could see him again. He'd disappeared for nearly fifteen minutes and the people at HBO Remote Control were ready to go in through the emergency hatch a second time.

But in the end, there was no need. By the time Starr made it down to the grand entranceway, the sun was up and the sealed front doors were open.

The Admiral was waiting on the porch. Rooney and Fisk were with him, as were the two marine sentries who'd been watching the only road into Happy Valley.

Starr gave them CPO Sterns' location and condition, leading Sergeant Fisk and the two marines to rush into the haunted house to rescue the missing SEAL.

Once they were gone, Hawley asked Starr: "Did he say anything about what happened?"

"He tried," Starr told him. "But I discouraged him, for his own good, plus who knew who could have been listening in. Just how the blood, the decapitation and everything else fits in, I don't know. But the guy was at the bottom of that stunt shaft all along. He's got a broken arm and he needs a bath, but he'll be OK."

Starr would learn later that it was Fisk who went back down the hidden stunt shaft and, after determining there was only one way out, stabilized Sterns, put him on his shoulders . . . and carried him back up the slide, where the two other marines were waiting.

"I'm sure Sterns will be able tell you the whole story once he gets patched up, sir," Starr concluded. "Plus, I'll send you my after-action report right away."

Hawley actually shook his hand. "Good work in there, lieutenant."

Starr was slightly shocked at the Admiral's gesture. "Just glad we were able to find the guy," he finally replied.

A black-camo Army medivac helicopter had already landed out on Spooky Street just across from the UFO Crash set, standing by to fly CPO Sterns to the nearest trauma center.

So, Starr's job here was done.

He was about to salute Hawley, then gracefully take his leave, drive home and collapse.

But the senior officer stopped him with a question: "What's the G-spot on your report going to say?"

He was referring to the space given to special investigators to fill in their personal opinions regarding the mission they'd just completed—Section G, AKA the G-Spot.

But the Admiral wanted to know his thoughts now.

So Starr told him.

"Again, just my opinion sir, but I think it's really time for someone to have a come-to-Jesus talk with HBO and especially whoever was running their special effects when this all happened. Whatever they were trying to do, they pulled it off brilliantly.

"The question is, what were they trying to do?"

Chapter Nine

Starr barely remembered driving back to San Diego.

Between the weekend traffic and his numbed-out state, he was amazed when he pulled into his building's parking lot that he hadn't nodded off somewhere along the way.

He waved to his doorman, Klaus, went up the elevator and fell into his apartment. Angel was waiting for him at the door; a long hug ensued.

She was dressed in a plain plaid shirt and nothing else; one of her many, sexy, hanging-around outfits. But despite his exhausted state, he knew she was supposed to be getting ready for a shoot in Los Salinas. Two hours' work, $40,000 an hour. She'd been looking forward to it for months.

He started to say something about it, but she touched his lips with her finger, then sat him down at the kitchen table and poured him a beer. A shoulders' massage came next. He was slowly returning to the real world.

But not for long.

"I have a few questions about the case," she said, digging her nails into him.

He drained the beer; she poured him another. "OK, such as?"

"We know the haunted house was re-wired by the TV crew," she began. "But very little of the interior was changed, right?"

"I guess," he said. "If you're trying to present a haunted house on the big screen, there's no real need to update it or do major renovations. I don't think people renovate haunted houses very often—even in Hollywood. They are what they are."

"I'm glad to hear you say that," she said.

She stood him up, led him by the hand through the wormhole, into her bedroom and to her laptop. Sitting him back down, she started a video downloaded from YouTube.

It was a very old western, black and white and silent.

"This is the movie I told you about, 'The Haunted Saddle,'" she said, just as the title appeared on the screen. "Made in 1927 . . ."

She fast forwarded to a scene between a cowboy and a bargirl with whom he'd just spent the night in the haunted house, looking for the missing ranch hand who happened to be her brother. They were standing in the familiar third-floor hallway, embracing.

Angel split the screen and called up the raw video feed from the haunted house that he'd sent her. Another quick search brought her to the part where the last two remaining SEALs were just getting to the third floor.

Remarkably, the camera angle in both videos was almost identical: looking straight down the hallway from the top of the stairs. The gallows was not in the "Haunted Saddle," but the big stained-glass window behind it was.

She put the videos in sync and then started both running together . . .

"Watch closely," she said. "What do you see?"

Starr put his beer aside and his nose almost touching the screen. But he saw nothing out of sorts.

She put the videos on a loop, and he watched them again.

Still nothing. Same with the third time.

Finally, she froze everything and pointed to the stained-glass window in the background of both.

"Look at the saddle," she said. "In the old movie, the horn, the seat and the cantle are going this way, right to left. It's the same in the raw feed—until . . ."

She fast forwarded to the point where Kurjan's helmet-cam was blinded by the flash of light which was the first indication that something was wrong with Sterns. The footage was shaky, but for a moment it showed a clear shot of the stained glass window in the background, Sterns' body violently wriggling below it.

"Now it's flipped," she said. "You can only see it for those couple seconds, before the live feed ends, but in those few moments, the saddle is definitely going in the other direction. In fact, the whole window is going the wrong way."

Starr watched it again—and she was right. He had her freeze it as a final confirmation. It didn't make sense, but in "The Haunted Saddle," the stain glass window is facing one way. In the raw feed during whatever the hell happened to Sterns, it's turned in the opposite direction.

Starr looked over at her, bewilderment on his face.

"So . . . what the heck are we saying here?" he asked.

She shrugged, looking very sweet as she did so. "Those last few seconds of the video feed showing the SEAL's head exploding must have come from somewhere else."

Starr drained his beer and immediately wanted a third one. "Could it be just some super CGI?" he asked, getting even closer to the screen.

"It doesn't look like CGI," Angel replied. "But even if it is, what's it doing in there? And why?"

"But where is that 'somewhere else?'" he asked. "Another studio? Another set—built to look *exactly* like Hell House?"

"Or at least the third floor of it," Angel replied. "What else could it be?"

Starr watched the loop three more times and then just shook his head.

"Damn," he said. "I've got to get back up there . . ."

Without another word, he went through the wormhole, but reappeared a minute later. He'd changed into all black clothes, including a black knit hat. He started to put on his coat.

But then Angel reappeared from her massive closet. She too was dressed all in black. Tight jeans, tight sweater, designer knit cap, hair pulled back.

Even her sneakers were black.

Incredibly sexy.

But he was confused. "Where are you going?"

"With you," she replied simply.

"But what about the Los Salinas shoot?"

She gently waved off his concerns.

"And miss what happens next?" she said, retrieving the Jag's keys. "No way . . ."

Chapter Ten

Angel drove.

While she kept it down to a respectable 95 MPH, she didn't need ESP or a police scanner to avoid getting a ticket. It was just in knowing that if she did get stopped and was recognized, the chances of the cop actually giving her a summons were pretty low.

Starr drank three cups of heavily sugared coffee along the way, this, his second mad dash north in as many days. In between sips, he told Angel the whole story again—this time with more detail. What happened to him inside the haunted house, fighting off the Ciggies, trying to avoid the FNFs, dealing with his own inner demons—and hearing somebody behind the walls.

As it turned out, his STPA2 kicked in just at the right moment, leading to him finding CPO Sterns at the bottom of the stunt shaft. That the guy was actually alive was astonishing and made going through it all worthwhile at least. He planned to include it all in his after-action report along with his belief that someone at HBO ginned up the whole thing as a publicity stunt.

But . . . there was this one last crazy thing that neither of them could understand. If HBO was behind it all, why would they even need a duplicate studio, depicting part of a duplicate Hell House, just to shoot the fake death scene?

And if such a place existed, where was it?

They reached the movie ranch just as the sun was beginning to set.

The marine guards were long gone; Angel sped past the old sign and down the dusty road unchallenged. Off to their left was the high-desert flat where the HBO Remote fort once stood. It, too, was gone.

They topped the last rise and from here were able to look down onto the movie set town. It appeared abandoned as well.

All in one day, everyone gone, Starr thought. Like nothing had ever happened here.

Angel slowed to a stop just before Gangster Ave and they surveyed the four blocks of movie sets up close. This would be their first hurtle. If their idea was to find some kind of phantom studio somewhere close by, they would have to get really lucky, because it would be virtually impossible for just the two of them to search the weird little town by themselves.

But with Starr's STPA2 not locked in, he tried another method.

He reached over and lightly touched Angel's forehead.

"If you were going to build a fake TV studio out here," he asked her, "where would you put it? Maybe 1930s Chicago? Dodge City? Bombed-out Berlin?"

She shivered dramatically for a moment, pretending to absorb some kind of superpower from him, when in reality, it was actually the reverse. At the same time, she was looking at an HBO street map app of Happy Valley; it listed all the individual set locations.

"This is the one I'd pick," she said, showing him the map.

The tip of her long red fingernail was resting on a site on Spooky Street a half block from Hell House and right next to a set labeled Crucifixion Hill.

The place was called "Lot 6—Mad Scientist Lab."

Starr leaned over and kissed her on the cheek.

"Of course," he said. "Where else would it be?"

They put on their own personal his-and-her NVGs, Angel pulling back her strawberry blonde hair to accommodate the gear.

She slowly drove past Hell House, now completely dark and, to Starr at least, looking even creepier than before.

Where the haunted house lot resembled a rundown 1930s Victorian mansion, the Mad Lab looked like a castle. Built of old fiberboard painted to look like stone and cement, it was a dreary gray structure with twin parapets and a tower. Block glass squeezed into ornamental window openings provided illumination from the outside world. Surround it with a half dozen enormous weeping willow trees to lend an even more mysterious air and you achieved the objective: This was a place where Frankenstein could have been born.

Angel doused the headlights, put the engine on noise-suppressed idle and approached the place cautiously.

"Something is happening out front," she reported. "A couple moving vans. See them?'

Starr did. "Six people, maybe seven or eight at the most. They don't look like HBO employees. Not as diverse. And they're moving stuff out. Kind of a strange time to be doing it, isn't it?"

Also, in evidence, oddly, were two grandstands; metal bleachers like seen in a school gymnasium. They were set up on the other side of the Mad Lab's driveway, facing its front doors.

"Are they expecting a crowd?" Starr wondered.

"Let's get closer," she said.

They parked the Jag on Gangster Ave. and made their way back to the Mad Lab. Past the Black Lagoon, across Spooky Street, through the graveyard in front of Hell House, then into the mansion's backyard.

Climbing to the top of Crucifixion Hill, they were able to hide behind a fallen, life-size wooden-mold cross. Under the cover of darkness, thanks to their NVGs, they could look right down on the Mad Lab front door, just 100 feet away.

They'd arrived in time to see one of the moving trucks getting its rear doors locked up, apparently full. The trucks looked like typical long-hall vans, but neither bore a name or logo. The people doing the moving were not in coveralls, but rather casual sportswear. They all had military-style haircuts as well—again, not very HBO-ish.

The men were carrying rubber containers out of the building; they resembled little bathtubs. Everything was covered, but because the NVGs were heat sensitive, Starr and Angel caught glimpses of electronic ghosts inside the tubs. Still-warm TV monitors, computers and other electronics—including video cameras.

Suddenly Angel's fingernails were digging into his arm. "This just got weirder," she said. "What's that behind the second moving truck?"

It was an ambulance, clearly marked as belonging to San Fernando Mercy General. But it looked abandoned, with a canvas drop cloth covering the front windshield.

"What's that doing here?" Starr said.

Angel was already punching her cellphone. She quickly came up with a startling piece of information.

"There is no San Fernando Mercy Hospital," she told him, indicating a list of hospitals in the area. Yet here was an ambulance bearing that exact name.

A moment later, Starr spotted something even stranger.

To the left of the front doors, hidden beneath one of the overhanging weeping willows, was an Army medivac helicopter. Starr told Angel he was certain it was the same aircraft he saw out on Spooky Street, on hand to pick up the injured SEAL, CPO Sterns.

"But where did it transport him to?" he said.

"My guess is a hospital in Dreamland called 'Mercy General,'" Angel replied, seeing the stashed copter.

Their attention went back to the people loading the moving truck. A trio of men came out of the building with three more tubs. They put them into the second moving truck, declared it full and closed up the back. While the rest of the movers climbed into the vans, the three men had a quick conversation.

The his-and-her NVGs were not equipped with the Super Ear app, so Starr and Angel couldn't hear what the three men were saying.

But it didn't matter—Angel could read lips.

"Your turn to drive." she reported one of them as saying. "'We'll get the rest in the morning.'"

Chapter Eleven

Starr and Angel waited thirty minutes after the two vans departed before they made their move.

Then, down Crucifixion Hill and right up to the front door of the Mad Lab, they could see no security alarm, and they'd noted none of the men paused to do anything like set one before they left. The door held nothing but a simple Yale lock and Starr was certain it wasn't insured by Lloyd's. His stiletto blade did the honors and in they went.

They found themselves in a dimly lit foyer. In front of them was a large open space with the remains of a laboratory movie set. Lots of beakers, Bunsen burners and test tubes. Lots of old lights and coils of thick electrical cables not used in decades.

This area was unlit. But looking to their left, they saw an open door at the end of the corridor, a dim light emanating from within.

Starr took out his Sig, and then put Angel behind him.

"Remember, you're not supposed to be here," he told her in a whisper as they started creeping down the hallway.

"I don't think either of us is," she whispered back.

Reaching the end of the corridor, they flattened themselves against the wall next to the door with the bare light streaming out. Starr flipped up his NVGs and peeked in.

What he saw at first seemed incomprehensible—but definite proof that their deduction had been right.

Inside was an exact recreation of the third floor of the Hell House.

It was all there. The long dark hallway, the prop gallows. The pull-down ladder. The stained-glass window behind it. And just like Hell House, above the fake ceiling were banks of movie lights, cameras and microphones. Everything had a crude, unfinished look. Anything that didn't have to be painted, wasn't.

"This is insane . . ." Angel breathed, looking into the room herself. "What is happening here?"

Starr's eyes immediately went to the stained-glass window. While it shouldn't have surprised him, it did.

"Look," he whispered to her. "The 'haunted saddle' is facing the wrong way."

"Just like in the video blip," she whispered back.

It *was* crazy . . . but suddenly some things started making sense.

"HBO, or someone, had to have built this place for the sole purpose of hacking into the live broadcast from Hell House," he said. "There's no other explanation."

"But why go through all this?" Angel asked. "It's just some stupid reality show."

"Maybe that's the point," Starr replied.

His ESP suddenly flashed—and it wasn't about anything good.

Hold on to her, quick . . .

Starr immediately put his arm around Angel and pulled her tight. Two seconds later, all the lights inside the set went out.

This was complete darkness. No high ceiling LEDs, no light anywhere. Their NVGs went black.

Starr held her tighter—both smart enough not to move, not to make a sound.

Then, voices, murmuring, echoing and distant, but getting closer. Starr felt a familiar chill go through him. He never needed to be reminded that dark buildings and disembodied voices did not mix well with him.

But these were not the voices of the dead.

A barrage of flashlights blinked on and they discovered eight armed men were walking towards them. It was the moving crew. But now they were carrying weapons —real M-4 rifles, not the fake HBO kind.

They stopped, and one man stepped forward and spoke for the rest.

"You two are not supposed to be in here," he told them politely.

Angel instantly took off her hat and let her hair down. Suddenly she was very recognizable. She introduced herself and then Starr as her assistant.

Studying her closely by the glow of his flashlight, the man seemed genuinely surprised to meet a famous model way out here.

"I'm doing a photo shoot for HBO somewhere around here next week," Angel lied sweetly. "I just wanted to get a vibe, you know?"

"I do," the man replied with a knowing chuckle.

"Now, this place," Angel went on. "It's creepy, but I'm not sure we're on the right set."

The guy laughed again. "I think you want the Haunted House lot," he said. "It's one block that way, just over the hill."

But Starr knew it wasn't going to be that easy—and he was right.

Because during the entire encounter, he and Angel were still wearing their his-and-hers NVGs. To emphasize this point, the man directed his flashlight from Angel's face to Starr's night vision goggles.

So before he or Angel could take a step towards the door, the man added: "But first—you'll have to come with us."

Chapter Twelve

Relieving them of his Sig and their NVGs, the man led them onto the fake Hell House set where he flipped a switch, once again dimly illuminating the hallway.

Even in their precarious position, Starr and Angel marveled at the detail of the ersatz third floor. It would have seemed impossible for a viewer to tell which location the Hell House show's video feed had been coming from.

Except for The Haunted Saddle.

Starr and Angel glanced at each other several times during this silent march, no need to talk, but stirring the same stew of thoughts and coming out with the same question:

Who did all this?

Once in the basement, they were brought to a small room that looked like an employees' lounge. TV, fridge, microwave, ugly furniture and old magazines, including a year-old copy of *LA Cosmo* with Angel on the cover.

Two familiar faces were inside—and they were an odd couple. Owens from HBO was on the couch, looking greatly annoyed, his clothes wrinkled. Sitting next to him, his heavily bandaged, plaster-cast right arm in a massive sling was SEAL CPO Butch Sterns.

Despite the gravity of the situation, their eyes went to Angel as soon as she walked in. Owens was quickly on his feet; Sterns close behind. Angel said quick hellos to them, Starr trying his best to shepherd her though the hasty greetings.

The man who had led them here waited until the introductions were over. Then he said: "Sorry for the inconvenience. You'll be OK here. It won't be long."

With that he backed out of the door and closed it behind him. The sound of a double lock clicking in place echoed through the tiny room.

"We are now officially in jail," Owens said, back to his prissy self. He looked to Starr, seeking a voice of reason.

"Can you please tell me what's going on here, lieutenant? These thugs picked me up more than six hours ago. No explanation. My family doesn't know where I am. And our hero here, CPO Sterns, has chosen this very moment to be tight-lipped."

It was Angel who actually replied. As gently as possible, she whispered to him: "He might know better than to talk openly in this situation."

It took a moment, but Owens got the message. These thugs, whoever they were, just built an exact recreation of the third floor of Hell House, less than a block over from the real place, for God-knows-what reason. Bugging this little clubhouse was certainly not beyond them.

"So we just sit here?" Owens asked Starr, his voice low.

Starr started to reply—but then froze. Angel thought he was going to sneeze. Instead, it was his STPA2 kicking in.

"Yes," he said after a moment. "We sit here and do nothing . . ."

Owens was very close to losing it. "And for how long?"

But Starr remained immobile. He didn't want to ruin anything. "For about five more seconds," he added.

Exactly five seconds later, they heard the lock turn in the room's door. It swung open and a man in full camo black combat suit with a large fritz helmet walked into the room.

They couldn't see his face, but Starr knew who he was. The man's hands were covered with grime. It was the marine who had stopped him at the entrance to the Happy Valley when he first got here.

So, he'd been in on it too.

"I'm really sorry for the inconvenience gentlemen— and ma'am," he said in that monotone jarhead way of speaking. "I'm afraid you've stumbled upon a classified operation, so we just have to detain you for just a while longer, and . . ."

But Owens wasn't hearing it.

He jumped up and was suddenly in the man's face—J Crew versus G.I. Joe.

"This is unlawful imprisonment," he began. "As a citizen of the United States, I demand that you release me, right now."

The marine with the dirty hands stayed cool. He looked down at Owens like a lizard contemplating a bug, just before the sticky tongue comes out.

"This is a national security issue," he said, trying to maintain a façade of friendliness. "And as a citizen myself, I want to thank you for your understanding and patience and . . ."

But even though this was happening, Starr's STPA2 never slowed down. He was hearing everything the marine was saying, but he was also somewhere else in time.

Somewhere just a few seconds ahead.

Owens turned around and confronted him and Sterns.

"You two are members of the military," he seethed at them. "Doesn't that mean anything anymore? You're supposed to defend our Constitution—instead you're literally going to do nothing?"

Starr suddenly announced: "Yes, we are . . ."

That was it. Owens was about to blow. But at that moment, Starr looked at Sterns, Sterns looked at Angel, who looked right back at Starr. She nodded to him.

"For about three more seconds . . ." he mouthed the words to all of them. It was just long enough for Angel to gently nudge Owens away from the closed door.

Three . . . two . . . one . . .

The door opened a crack, and someone tossed in a combination flash and concussion grenade; it's called a Double Willy—twice the brightness, twice the bang! In the same instant, CPO Sterns launched himself off the couch and viciously body-slammed the marine with the dirty hands, his plastered right arm hitting the guy square in the jaw. The marine hit the floor with a thud, out cold.

"Lock the door behind you next time, a-hole . . ." Sterns berated the unconscious man. "And wash your fucking hands . . ."

By the time Starr could see again, and it was just barely, he found Admiral Hawley was standing in front of him. Watching his six was Commander Rooney. Both were carrying M-4s. Real ones . . .

Starr started to say *how did you get here*, when he realized he was temporarily deaf too. Hawley realized this, so he pointed to his ears and then mouthed the words to Starr: "Form up. We're leaving . . ."

But then the Admiral's eyes fell on Angel—and the senior officer paused a moment.

"And are you Lieutenant Starr's . . ." he said, before running out of words. An awkward moment at a strange time.

Angel heard him, just barely, and saved him. "I'm Lieutenant Starr's next-door neighbor," she said. "And I feel like I should salute you or something."

"Not necessary," Hawley babbled. "Let's go . . ."

On that, out the door they went.

At the same moment, two members of the moving crew were walking in the hallway outside, each carrying a cup of coffee, real weapons nowhere in sight.

Hawley and Rooney hit them two seconds after coming out of the room. Bowled over, hot coffee spilling everywhere, the men collided, cracking their skulls and knocking each other out. Owens side-stepped the two fallen men and took off running. Behind him were Starr, Angel and Sterns. They ran *over* the pair—and kept right on going too.

It was only about fifty feet to the front doors. But on reaching the expansive laboratory set, they stumbled upon six more men having a coffee break. It was the rest of the moving crew. They were surprised to see the prisoners had broken out, but reacted quickly.

They'd been gathered near the front doors, sitting in circle of old metal folding chairs. Now, they all rose as one, blocking the only way out. Still, as the two groups came face to face, one of the men raised his hands as if to say, let's talk this over.

But Hawley had other ideas.

The Admiral threw a massive left hook that hit the guy so hard, he bounced twice—once off the cardboard wall behind him and once when he hit the floor. A moment later, Rooney delivered a haymaker to the man next in line. But it was thrown with such velocity, it caused both the puncher and the punch-ee to topple over into a heap.

Owens took the next swing, missed, tripped and found himself in the middle of a scrum. Starr jumped in, as did the four remaining crew cuts, and just like in a western movie, the fight was on.

Starr was at an advantage here. A couple Navy shrinks thought his STPA2 might be triggered by adrenaline rushes, and at this moment, it would seem they were right. As soon as the first punches were thrown, he found himself in that strange world of pre-cog shrinkage. Everything was slightly blurred, slightly surreal—and slightly ahead of itself. When one of the bad guys started to line him up for a punch, Starr was not only able to duck the blow, but he also hit the guy in the jaw and then kicked him in the beans, causing him to roll away in agony.

Then Starr pulled a guy off Owens' back, so Owens could get off Rooney's back. But once Rooney was up on his feet, the ferocity of the fight suddenly intensified. He and Hawley began swinging their M-4s like clubs. Their opponents, weapons out of reach, employed the metal folding chairs as shields, forcing back the two Navy officers, only to lose ground again. Back and forth, up and down, it had devolved into medieval warfare.

While *this* was going on, CPO Sterns body-slammed the moving crew guy closest to the door. Knocked off his feet, his head bounced repeatedly between a plaster cast and the sawdust-covered floor, the victim went from bloody to unconscious in seconds. Sterns completed the assault by picking the man up, and with one hand, depositing him in a trash barrel. Only then did Starr realize who the beaten man was: Chief Master Donn Kurjan, the second in line SEAL during the Hell House incident. The guy whose stumbling, bumbling camera recorded Sterns' gruesome but fake death. The guy who spilled the fake blood onto the gallows.

He'd been whisked away by the HBO first responders, raving like a maniac, or so it seemed. But Kurjan had been in on it all along—as his former SEAL-brother Sterns had just figured out. Thus, the internecine skull cracking. Just like the people they were currently trading punches with, the ambulance, the medivac helicopter and God knew what else, nothing was real here. Nothing, and nobody, was what they seemed.

It felt like the brawl went on forever, but it lasted no longer than thirty seconds. Punches landing, the sounds of bones crunching, random cursing at high volume, it ended when Angel became involved—and in a most unusual way. One of the bad guys was about to unload on Owens when she calmly reached over and gave him a finger squeeze to the shoulder. The man collapsed immediately.

Even amidst the chaos, Hawley took a moment to tell Starr: "You've got quite a neighbor there."

The escapees finally prevailed. Of their six opponents, three were unconscious and the other three were making it clear they didn't want to play anymore.

It became very quiet inside the fake castle.

"We have a vehicle nearby," Hawley told Starr. "It will be tight, but it will carry all of us out of here. My plan is to get out of Happy Valley, contact the nearest law enforcement base. Go to that location, and then call the Pentagon and find out exactly what the hell is going on out here."

"I'm all for that, sir," Starr replied.

Hawley went over to the building's front door; Rooney beside him. Their M4s were up and ready for anything.

Hawley signaled that they'd go out first, and the rest should follow. He received thumbs-up from all around.

On that, the Admiral drew a deep breath, and opened the castle's door.

Chapter Thirteen

As the last one out, Angel had the best view of what happened next.

It began with a brilliant flash of light. It hit them like a silent explosion as soon as they opened the door.

But it wasn't a flash grenade. There was no big *bang!*

This light wasn't blinding. It was dazzling.

Angel knew this illumination. Knew its warmth. She'd walked countless fashion runways. Their lights always looked, always felt, like this.

Dazzling . . .

TV lights . . .

Then she saw the audience. The two grandstands, empty when they first went into the building, were now full. The lights prevented her from seeing just who was sitting in the gallery, but they were waving pennants and she could hear them doing a quasi-syncopated cheer.

All this was evident in a matter of seconds—still, it took another few heartbeats to sink in.

"Oh my God," she whispered urgently, grabbing Starr's arm and *really* digging in her nails. "We're on TV . . ."

The escapees stopped dead in the lights, frozen by their glare. Owens began swearing. He knew these dazzling lights too.

"How the fuck is this happening?" he said. "No one told me about this . . ."

Two figures emerged from behind the brightness. One was wearing a 007 style tuxedo and carrying a microphone. Behind him was someone dressed in a football mascot's costume, specifically a mule. They were carrying a hand-held camera. Some very cheesy band music began playing in the background. It was actually a march by John Phillips Sousa called "The Caissons Song," better known as the official anthem of the U.S. Army.

The music grew so loud, and the crowd so rambunctious, the man with the microphone had to nearly shout to be heard by the escapees.

"We're sorry," he began earnestly. "But you've just been punked by the U.S. Army special projects support group. It's part of the pregame show package they are airing before the Army-Navy game next week. Now, we're about to go live—so can you all look surprised?"

***

The lights, the music, the action—none of it lasted very long.

In fact, it went on for exactly fifteen more seconds. Just enough for the donkey to get his shot of the startled escapees and then pan back to the tuxedoed announcer in time for him to say, in that game-show host sort of way: "Wait until you see what the Army caught the Navy doing out here! How will Navy return the favor? We'll find out right after this . . ."

Then the dazzle dimmed, and Starr was able see again—but as always, nothing was as it seemed.

The couple dozen people in the grandstands shown waving Army pennants and making a lot of noise, climbed out of their civilian-looking clothes to reveal each was clad in a black-camo uniform bearing no name, rank or insignia. Scanning their faces, Starr could tell they were not regular military, simply because there were no young troopers in the group.

These guys were veterans. Ex-special ops, he guessed, now under contract to . . . who?

Certainly not the U.S. Army's Athletic Department.

These men began disassembling the lights and camera equipment. The announcer gave his microphone to his mule friend and then sidled up to the Admiral.

"Sorry about this, sir," he half-whispered. "My dad was in submarines and . . ."

But Hawley cut him to the quick. "This has nothing to do with Army-Navy football, does it?" he seethed at the man.

Taken back, the man sheepishly shook his head no.

"That's all just eyewash, sir," he said, sounding chastened. "You guys just wandered into an exercise that's all, so they needed a backstop story. Not the first time it's happened."

Translation: Eyewash meant changing the reality of something by manipulating documents, video and so on. A backdrop story was something concocted to falsely explain what you were doing in the first place. Both were trademarks of very, very secret operations.

"Whose exercise is it?" Hawley asked the guy.

But the man just shook his head. "That's above my pay grade, sir," he said. "But I can take you to someone who'll be able to explain it all."

The small group followed the man around to the front of the Mad Lab, back across Cowboy Street and down to Berlin Square.

Here was parked a caravan of RVs and house trailers of all shapes and sizes. Hardly rock-star style tour buses, these vehicles were so ordinary they would blend in on any road, street or highway in America.

They were taken to a large Airstream trailer and brought inside. The interior was laid out like a war room. A military planning table was at its center. Surrounding it were a dozen video monitors showing everything from the front door of Mad Lab to a live satellite feed coming from who knew where. Combined, it made it seem like this little cabin was hooked into the entire rest of the planet.

A man was sitting at the planning table, his back to the group. He was having a hushed but animated conversation with someone via Bluetooth.

The group heard him say: "OK—you lead, I'll follow . . ." and then end the conversation.

Only then did he turn around—and suddenly, Starr felt another piece of the puzzle fall into place.

This was the guy who'd been running it all, right from the start. Always there. Always helpful. Even heroic. Hearing and seeing everything, while hardly saying a word of his own.

Sergeant Fisk, driver, USMC . . .

They all gasped on seeing him—except for Angel who didn't know who he was.

"I'm really sorry for the inconvenience gentlemen— and lady," Fisk began, his movie star good looks seeming to have aged in just the past day; he looked much older now than Starr would have guessed. "I'm afraid you've stumbled upon a classified operation. Four of you are service members—and I'm sure your two friends here, Mister Owens and Miss Angel Kleinpeter-Morosi, respect your point of view. So, believe me, the easiest way to get out of here, is to sign these documents."

He handed an inch-thick binder to Hawley. It contained nondisclosure agreements and security waivers, to be expected. But it also contained releases from HBO saying that everyone in the group knew beforehand that they were taking part in an entertainment-style video hyping the upcoming Army-Navy game.

Hawley read this particular document and nearly exploded.

"But this is nonsense," he told Fisk. "None of us had anything to do with anything like this."

Fisk just nodded. "I know," he said simply. "That's just a little insurance policy. We have to cover all bases."

"So if we squawk?" Hawley asked him.

Fisk just shrugged. "Those documents find their way to TMZ, along with that video we just shot of you leaving the Mad Lab."

"And goodbye credibility," Rooney said, especially upset that Fisk had fooled him even more so than he did the others.

Fisk shrugged again. "We all have jobs to do," he replied.

But Hawley was growing more agitated by the moment.

"So, you and your little boy scout troop here are . . . what?" he demanded of Fisk. "Disinformation agents?"

Fisk shrugged a third time and repeated: "We all have jobs to do . . ."

"What if we don't sign?" Starr asked him.

"The same thing happens," Fisk replied. "We can produce documents containing your signatures that can fool any handwriting expert. But, of course, we'd like you to sign voluntarily."

"Well, how about if the four of us beat your brains in?" CPO Sterns asked him angrily. They had a problematic relationship. Even though it was Fisk who carried him out of the pit, he was also responsible for the fake floor swallowing Sterns up and dumping him there in the first place.

"Sure, that's one road we can take," Fisk replied evenly. "But where does something like that lead? We have a fight here. You escape again—but we'll just catch up to you, and we can have another fight if you want, but it's always going to end the same way. And that way is Groundhog Day—until you come around to our position on things."

He took a breath then continued: "I'll be straight with you guys—and you, ma'am. All I really need is just one person to sign-off and then we can put the rest of you down as malcontents or something."

Fisk turned to Owens and spoke directly to the HBO exec. "These four men are part of the military—they have to obey orders. But you're a civilian. This really has nothing to do with you. Your best move would be to sign and then you can be on your way and we can pretend like nothing happened. We're through out here. We're not coming back. So why wouldn't you do it?"

Owens did not move. He stayed frozen.

Suddenly, it was all up to him.

Suddenly, it was he who could tip the balance one way or the other.

Fisk thought he saw an opening, so he repeated his last question: "Why wouldn't you do it?"

Owens stared back at him. He kept his arms crossed and never lost the prissy scowl, but when the moment came, he rose to the occasion . . . and became an unexpected patriot.

"Why wouldn't I do it?" he replied to Fisk, almost choking on the words. "Because this is still the United States of America, that's why."

More gasps around the room—Fisk included. He might have been the most surprised of all. Unable to contain herself, Angel walked over to Owens and embraced him.

She whispered in his ear: "Thank you . . ."

And that was it. It was like all the air went out of the room. Fisk looked like he couldn't believe what he was hearing. But he pivoted quickly to a kind of Plan B.

Turning back to Hawley, he said: "Admiral, you must understand my position. We're dealing with an SCI mission here."

SCI stood for sensitive compartmentalized information, or better put, an extremely classified operation.

"I mean, yes, it's covered with static," he continued. "But at its core, we're really working something here."

But Hawley was tired, he was hungry, he was thirsty, plus he'd just been in his first fistfight since the Academy. Moreover, in his mind, Fisk was the reason he was not in Hawaii right now.

"I can sympathize with you, *Sergeant Fisk*," Hawley replied, intentionally drawing out the last two words even though he knew it was highly unlikely that Fisk was just a sergeant, or that his name was even Fisk. "But I don't think I'm talking too much out of turn by saying we all second what our friend, Mister Owens just said. Unless you tell us who you are working for, we've got a problem."

Another tense silence descended on the trailer.

The wheels were turning so fast in Fisk's head, he was getting flushed. Finally, he relented—sort of . . .

"OK, Admiral, I will share that information," he said. "But only with you. And after you're briefed, I'll leave it up to you if you think it's in the national interest to inform the others."

The ball back in their court, Hawley looked to the small group. They all felt the same way. No one wanted any part of a Groundhog Day situation—and something was better than nothing."

"We'll wait for you, Admiral," Starr said as the others began filing out of the RV.

"Count on it," Sterns spit at Fisk as he walked by, even though it was he who carried Sterns out of the pit.

Once again, Angel was the last out the door, now arm-in-arm with Owens.

"And next time," she told Fisk in that Angel kind of way, sweet but devastating, "try to get the saddle right . . ."

Chapter Fourteen

The sun rose, the stars blinked out and it started to warm up in the San Fernando Valley.

Starr and Angel were back up on Crucifixion Hill, sitting on the remains of the old prop cross. Rooney and Sterns were with them, as was Owens. Two of the mysterious uniformed men were nearby, keeping an eye on them.

Around 7 a.m. two men emerged from the Mad Lab wearing pilot uniforms. Together, they pulled the Army medivac copter out from under the weeping willows and started its engines. Three of the eight men who'd lost the fight inside the Mad Lab earlier were led out and put on board.

The man who'd played the part of the TV emcee, finally out of his tuxedo, climbed the hill and offered to airlift Sterns to the nearest military hospital. The injured SEAL agreed to go only after Rooney volunteered to go with him.

There were salutes, but then hugs all around. Starr exchanged contact information with both men and Angel promised to send each an autographed cover of *LA Cosmo*.

The copter took off and all was quiet again.

***

It was 8 a.m. when the Airstream trailer, being pulled by a Dodge Hemi 440 truck, arrived on Spooky Street and drove up to the Mad Lab's front door.

It remained there, silent and still, for about ten minutes. Finally, the door opened and Admiral Hawley stepped out. With that, the truck and trailer drove away.

The navy officer took a deep breath, straightened himself out—and began walking up Crucifixion Hill. But looking down at the man approaching, Starr didn't need his ESP to know he was carrying the weight of the world on his shoulders.

"Damn," he whispered to Angel, sitting right next to him. "This doesn't look good."

They both rose to meet him, but the Admiral walked over to Owens first. He shook the man's hand, had a few private words, then motioned Starr and Angel to join the conversation. Seeing the Admiral up close only confirmed Starr's previous diagnosis. The normally robust and frankly intimidating bulldog of a man suddenly looked very gaunt and pale.

"I just spent a good amount of time talking about you, Mister Owens," Hawley began. "And you're going to have to believe what I'm going to tell you on blind faith. Because that's all I can offer you."

Somehow, Owens understood.

"I will believe you," he replied, "because I think you are a man of integrity."

But the words seemed to physically hurt the senior Navy officer.

"You might not feel that way after I tell you all this," he replied. "But what is, just is. So here goes.

"You will be getting a government defense grant for $100 million. That's to pay off Lloyds and any losses HBO might have incurred in all this and I'm sure, with some left over. In return, the agency providing this grant asks that you don't reveal what happened here for at least fifty years."

"But I'm fifty now," Owens said.

Hawley managed a weak smile. "Exactly . . ."

He looked up at Starr and Angel and then continued.

"Number two, this agency will provide HBO with a second government defense grant, with you as the executor, to demolish the haunted house and the Mad Lab, and build two new ones exactly like them in their place."

This puzzled them all—especially Owens. "Why would the government want me to tear down these two structures and build new ones? What's the catch?"

Hawley seemed to be running out of gas. "Well, I guess you'll find out," he replied.

Owens thought for a few moments and then asked: "Are there papers that have to be signed to do all this?"

Hawley actually put his hand on the man's shoulder. "This is where you'll have to take that leap of faith, OK?"

"OK . . ."

Hawley took in another breath and measured his words before he spoke them.

"This agency, the one that is going to give you all this money, already has your signature on all the necessary documents as well as a video of you accepting their offers and signing those agreements."

All three of them looked back at Hawley now.

Owens began to say "How?" but Hawley cut him off.

"You should be very proud of what you did back there, Mister Owens," he told the HBO exec. "I'm proud just to have known you, as screwed up as all this was. But as someone who has been in and out of these kinds of black ops before, my advice is: Take the money and keep the secret."

A long silence ensured. Nobody spoke a word. Starr knew if they could take the wind out of Hawley's sails, then these guys must be deeper than deep.

As it turned out, Owens never really agreed to anything, not verbally anyway. He just sort of shrugged and nodded. On that, Hawley signaled the two men in black camos who'd been watching the group atop Crucifixion Hill.

"These guys will drive you to the National Guard armory where your people have been staying," Hawley told him. "I trust them, so you can trust them. Once you're back with your group, these guys will then make arrangements to get you all where you all need to go."

Again, Owens never really agreed; he just shrugged again and then awkwardly shook hands with the Admiral.

"Thank you, sir," he said. "I'm proud to have known you, too."

That's when Hawley did something that greatly surprised Starr and almost brought tears to Angel's eyes.

Hawley saluted him.

Owens was tempted to salute back, but he chose to shake the admiral's hand again. Then he did the same with Starr, telling him: "If you ever want spitball series ideas, just look me up."

Starr assured him he would.

Then Owens turned to Angel. He was almost shaking at this point. The next moment promised to be the most awkward yet, but then Angel did what she did best.

She stepped forward and embraced Owens tightly. And he hugged back. Angel whispered something in his ear and then kissed him.

Owens at least knew the importance of a graceful exit. So he did a kind of half bow to her, nodded to Starr and Hawley—and then he joined the two men and went down the hill to a waiting GMC truck. He gave them one last look up on the hill, one last wave and then he was gone.

Now it was just the three of them. Starr began to ask Hawley the big question, but before he could even speak, the Admiral beat him to the punch.

The senior officer just looked him straight in the eye and said: "DARPA . . ."

Starr collapsed back to his seat on the cross.

"Dar—who?" Angel asked.

"Defense Advanced Research Projects Agency . . ." Hawley said, being careful to get every word right.

Angel looked to Starr for a translation.

"The Pentagon's mad scientists," he told her simply. "Appropriately enough. They're not a classified operation, because they don't have to be. It's the missions they run with other people. They can be deeper than deep."

"And maybe even deeper than that," Hawley chimed in.

"Are these the guys who invented the Internet?' Angel asked after a moment.

"Yes, they did," Starr told her. "That and a lot of other things—a lot of them very crazy."

"Such as?" she wanted to know.

Starr shrugged. "Self-guiding bullets. Robot insects. Spy bugs . . ."

"Flying submarines," Hawley added. "Exoskeletons. Mechanical elephants . . ."

"Mind control. Remote viewing. Brain chips . . ."

"Sounds like you could go on and on," Angel said. "But what are they doing out here?"

"It's a DARPA experiment to hack into a TV broadcast without being detected," Hawley said gravely. "No matter what they say, that's what they were doing . . ."

Starr was shocked. "But isn't that illegal?"

"Just about everywhere around the world but the United States," was Hawley's reply.

A brief silence, then Angel asked: "But what's to stop us from just calling CNN or someone and telling them everything?"

"Because they've got 'proof' that we agreed to this all along," Hawley replied, using air quotes. "Just like they doctored a video showing Owens signing his soul away to them, they can prove we did something that we didn't. And that means, talking about it to anyone would be a violation of the Security Act. The government tends to go harsh if you're convicted of that."

Starr and Angel exchanged worried looks, but then Starr said: "It might take a while, but we could break out of that. Get someone to listen to us and hear what really happened."

Hawley was nodding, but not in a good way.

"I admire your pluck, lieutenant," he said. "But in addition to all the forged nondisclosure agreements and security waivers and release forms, all of them with our signatures, having us agree to be on this football video thing, they've also got sensitive security data, on all of us. Plus, they have extensive personal data on all of us too—and our families. The implication being they can make it go away with the click of a mouse, or even worse, it could be altered."

Starr was closing in on his boiling point. "But you don't think they've got the juice to get us tossed out of the Navy, do you?" he asked the Admiral.

Hawley suddenly went pale again. "Believe me, they can do that and even worse."

"Worse as in how, sir?"

Hawley looked up—first at Angel and then back at Starr.

"Well, let me put his delicately, lieutenant," he said. "Do you own a Superman costume?"

Both Starr and Angel turned red. Hawley just nodded slowly.

"These guys know everything about everybody," he said darkly.

Yet another long silence. Starr looked down at the Mad Lab and then back at Hawley.

"And what is their explanation for all this?" he asked, exasperated. "I mean, what the hell were they *really* doing out here?'

Hawley just shook his head. "I really don't know," he said, looking back at the Mad Lab castle himself. "But dropping in that one bloody shot wasn't all they were up to. They were also slipping subliminal messages into the show. I'm guessing just about every time a flash grenade went off, and the screen went blank for a couple seconds, they slipped something in. Quick, just a micro-second, but just enough to cause digestive distress. You got a little queasy watching that raw tape even before CPO Sterns' head exploded, right?"

"It still feels off, sir," Starr replied. "But again, why go through all this when with about ten minutes on a CGI computer you could recreate a virtual TV set that would almost be indistinguishable from the real thing—especially since it's on the screen just a few seconds."

Hawley just shrugged. "Again, I don't know—proof of concept maybe?" he replied. "Or maybe they're testing this for someone who doesn't have access to multi-million dollar CGI computers but can do stuff with hammers and nails. Or is on a laptop in a cave somewhere."

Angel got his meaning right away. "This is very dangerous."

Hawley looked down at the ground for a moment.

"I can't disagree," he said finally. "Think of it. They're a government agency who has just proven to anyone in the know that they can manipulate mass media without getting caught. They had us running around like fools for two days because we saw CPO Sterns' head blow up. But what if they can quietly hack into a news broadcast and just twist it a little bit this way? A little bit that way? Or maybe break into the financial channels and just change a few numbers on the screen real quick—and then get out. And don't get caught?"

"Or, they want to get caught," Angel said softly. "Catch one or two people doing it and millions will never believe what they see on TV again. It will be *real* Fake News. People barely believe what they see now."

"If the credibility of the entire mass media takes a nose dive like that," Starr said, "and it never comes back? That's more power than a thousand ICBMs."

"And I don't want any part of it," Hawley said. "I gave my thirty plus years and I can truthfully say I didn't care who was in the White House."

He thought quietly for a few more moments, then added: "But now, so many things have changed. It's not the same country anymore. Not the same world. And I don't want to be associated with either one."

He thought another moment before reaching up to his shirt collar and removing his admiral's bars.

He handed them to Angel. "Can I ask you a favor, my dear?"

She took them tightly in her hand, confused but melting away in that Angel kind of way.

"Anything," she told him with heavenly sweetness.

"Hold on to these for me," he said. "Maybe someday I'll want them back. If that day comes, I'll get in touch with the lieutenant."

Then he added with a weak smile: "And he can just run next door and give you the message, if that's OK?"

She took his hand in hers—just for a moment—and said: "It's very OK . . ."

He shook hands with Starr. "I want to thank you, lieutenant," he said. "It was strange, but I guess that's what you do."

He lowered his voice and said: "Whatever superpowers you have, please be careful who you use them for . . ."

He hugged Angel and she hugged back.

Then he started back down the hill.

"But where are you going to go, sir?" Starr called after him.

"Honolulu," Hawley called back over his shoulder. And I'll swim there this time if I have to."

Chapter Fifteen

It was a long drive home.

Starr was behind the wheel; Angel was asleep twenty minutes in.

He hit the late morning traffic, and then road construction, and then more traffic in the early afternoon. They passed a minor accident, being attended to by the CHiPs that nevertheless had attracted a gaggle of media trucks, needlessly confusing things and adding even greatly to the traffic woes.

When they finally arrived home, it was raining and it was dark. Starr gently woke Angel and guided her to their building's lobby. He ran back to get her things and park the Jag.

When he returned, Angel was in a deep and hushed conversation with their doorman, Klaus.

The lobby was dim, now under the dull glare of muted LED lights. But way down the very end of the entry way, on one of the couches, they could see a figure, covered by a blanket, obviously asleep.

"Been here most of the day," Klaus explained, in German-tinged English. "Nice enough, but insisted they wait until you got back . . ."

Starr and Angel approached quietly, Klaus bringing up the rear. Starr reached down and very gently tapped the person on the shoulder.

They were instantly awake. Blanket flying, up on two feet, one hand habitually going to a back-pocket holster.

Black, low-cut sweater, black-and-red tartan mini-skirt, black tights and black boots this time—but the flaming red hair was still the same and so was the gold crucifix chain.

That Hibernian cuteness.

Those neon blue eyes.

It was Maura McCann.

Republic of Ireland, Special Detective Squad.

She looked up at Starr and then Angel and then back to Starr.

"We have to talk, Lieutenant Starr," she said to him, shaking his hand in a very professional way. "Because we've finally figured out how Father Friendly was able to win all that money in the first place . . ."

Coming June 2020!

BATTLE OF THE WINGMEN
Book 20
in
Mack Maloney's Best-Selling Wingman Series

Wingman and his United American allies take the newly re-built aircraft carrier, USS USA, on its first Pacific patrol, looking for a mystery fighter jet last seen flying over Los Angeles. Like Jason and the Argonauts, they have many adventures and fight numerous battles, until they find the mystery airplane, a discovery which leads to a dogfight for the ages.

For more information visit Mack at:

www.SpeakingVolumes.us

www.ingramcontent.com/pod-product-compliance
Lightning Source LLC
Chambersburg PA
CBHW020554260626
47157CB00003B/694